pictures
in the
dark

pictures in the dark

by

PATRICIA McCORD

BLOOMSBURY

Published by Bloomsbury, New York and London
Distributed to the trade by Holtzbrinck Publishers, LLC

Library of Congress Cataloging-in-Publication Data
McCord, Patricia.
Pictures in the dark / by Patricia McCord.
p. cm.
Summary: Life with their mentally ill mother becomes unbearable for
twelve-year-old Sarah and fifteen-year-old Carlie as they are deprived of
food and forbidden to use the bathroom.
ISBN 1-58234-848-0 (alk. paper)
[1. Sisters—Fiction. 2. Family problems—Fiction. 3. Child abuse—Fiction. 4.
Mental illness—Fiction.
5. Mothers and daughters—Fiction.] I. Title.
PZ7.M47841433Pi 2004
[Fic]—dc22
2003056252

Type set in Sabon Roman
Designed by Marikka Tamura

Printed in the U.S.A.
1 3 5 7 9 10 8 6 4 2

Bloomsbury USA Children's Books
175 Fifth Avenue
New York, New York 10010

All papers used by Bloomsbury Publishing are natural, recyclable products
made from wood grown in well-managed forests. The manufacturing
processes conform to the environmental regulations of the country of origin.

*For my sister, Brenda Dickinson,
the person who knows me best.*

ACKNOWLEDGMENTS

Many people had a hand in the creation of this book by reacting
to early chapters. Thanks to Carole Adler, Barbara Berger,
C. B. Christiansen, Kathryn Galbraith, Nancy Luenn,
Pete Mauser, Ruth Maxwell, Jane Morse Thompson, and my
husband, Bob McCord. Thanks also to the wonderful people at
Bloomsbury Children's Books, including Victoria Wells Arms and
Kate Kubert, who have set a new standard for author-publisher
relationships. In addition, three people added invaluable expert-
ise: Lt. Dan Malet of the Bothell, Washington, Police Department;
Chuck Rhoads of the Washington State Patrol; and Nancy Gale
Compau of the Spokane Public Library, Northwest Room.

one

AUTUMN, 1954.

"What'd you get, Carlie?" Sarah Neville whispered. She and her fifteen-year-old sister were supposed to be in bed, but Carlie moved soundlessly across the bedroom floor, casting shadows on the slanted ceiling.

"Not much," Carlie whispered back. "Just bread and some raisins. Turn on the light for a sec, will you?"

"No, they'll see it." Sarah sat wrapped in a blanket, keeping watch through the grated vent to the rooms below. Their parents were down there, just out of sight, sitting in front of the new television set.

Sarah wiped her nose on a crumpled piece of newspaper. "Did you get me any Kleenex?"

Carlie pulled a single piece out of her pocket and handed it to her.

A sore throat had developed earlier, and now Sarah's nose was runny, too. She took the tissue

7

gratefully and blew. "It's so cold up here; but I'm not sick, not yet, at least."

"Good," Carlie said. "I was going to get you an orange, but there was only one."

Sarah heard Dad mumble downstairs and shift in his big old chair, making it squeak. When he was home, she figured nothing really terrible would happen, nothing like what had happened last spring; but the girls were already breaking several of their mother's rules, and they knew better than to make noise or turn on the lights.

Carlie felt along the walls. "Here it is—got it," she whispered. Outlined in the glow from the living room, she lifted out a loose square of wallboard at the foot of her bed and stashed the food.

Bread and raisins. Sarah had been hoping for something more interesting, like Oreos or even one of the bottles of Coca-Cola she'd seen on the screened-in back porch, but this would fill them up. She pulled the blanket with her and stretched out on her stomach. Warm air from the room below bathed her face.

"Hurry, Carlie, Riley's on next." Sarah peered through the grate, trying to get a glimpse of the gray screen, then sat up abruptly. "Quick, she's coming!" A hint of someone's shadow was just moving out of view beneath her, heading for the kitchen and their door at the bottom of the stairs.

Carlie slipped around the end of her bed and

lowered herself onto her mattress. The door banged open. A rectangle of light shot up the stairs.

Then silence. Someone was listening at the bottom—it had to be her.

Sarah's ears strained for the sound of slippers on the stairs. Her heart pounded. In her brain, a flash: she saw an ugly rope of a bathrobe strap sliding almost gently out of its loops, then Carlie turning purple.

If their mother came charging up the stairs, Sarah knew she would go numb with fear, and then later she'd be overwhelmed with shame for being so afraid. What kind of a twelve-year-old was afraid of her own mother?

"Tt!" The sound their mother made with her tongue meant the girls weren't worth her trouble. Good. Sarah let out her breath. The slit of light narrowed and disappeared; the door at the bottom closed.

Footsteps moved back through the kitchen, then Sarah saw the top of a head with its tight black curls come into view beneath the grate.

"I've had it with those two." She passed into the living room. A saucer rattled, followed by a loud slurping sound that seemed to punctuate her irritation.

Dad's chair squeaked, but he didn't comment. He never seemed to notice their mother's meanness. Or maybe when he finally got home late at night, he was too tired to care. By then all he wanted to do was sit with her and smile and nod. He rarely did so much as come to their door. Even he understood the rules.

Sarah moved to her own bed, where she shivered between the chilly sheets. "She won't be back now," she said, pulling the covers tightly around her. "We can eat." The music announcing *The Life of Riley* drifted up through the vent.

Carlie got up again and opened their cupboard behind the wall. "We'd better have half and save the rest." She handed doll dishes to Sarah: a tiny cup full of raisins and a plate with a half slice of soft bread broken into several pieces. At twelve and fifteen they were too old to play with dolls, but the dishes came in handy on nights like this.

They would eat and listen to the TV, even if they couldn't see it. Sarah squeezed her bread into a sticky ball and sniffed it, savoring the delicious smell of yeast. She was plenty hungry now, but it would get worse if there were no breakfast in the morning. Sometimes their mother called them down for a bowl of cereal, and sometimes she seemed to forget they even lived there.

Sarah chewed the doughy ball and swallowed it down into the pit of her stomach. With it settled a small, warm seed of comfort. In spite of her runny nose and feeling closed off, she loved the safety of their tiny bedroom, built into the pointed top of the two-story house. The walls and ceiling were covered with one-foot squares of wallboard where she and Carlie could pin artwork, special school papers and pictures of movie stars. Being trapped upstairs never bothered Sarah as much as it did Carlie, maybe because she still had someone big to take care of her: Carlie herself.

Slanted to match the pitch of the roof, the ceiling leaned over two dark-green poster beds on opposite sides of the room. Only between the beds, in the middle of the room, could anyone stand up to full height.

In the front end of the room were large paned windows that opened like doors out over the roof. In the back, a small window overlooked the backyard, the alley beyond and the Phillips 66 gas station. Descending at a steep angle past the back window, the narrow flight of stairs dropped to the kitchen below.

Dividing the room almost in half was a white brick chimney that came up out of the floor and rose through the ceiling. Often the girls propped their pillows against the bricks and took in the warmth from the coal furnace far below in the basement.

Sarah chewed the raisins one at a time, feeling around with her finger to find the last one. I am *not* getting sick, she commanded herself.

On television, Riley and his wife were arguing. Carlie snickered. A beer commercial came on.

Sarah stared into the darkness, wondering how they had gotten here—to the point where they lived upstairs and stole food. It had been this way as far back as Sarah could reach. Did other families have secrets like theirs? Surely they didn't.

Sarah had been only two when they moved to Spokane. Carlie said back in Kentucky there had been relatives and birthday parties and trips to the park. She said their mother had smiled all the time then. But Sarah had been too young to remember, so it was the same as never happening.

All she knew was the mother who lived downstairs listening, watching and waiting for them to break her rules or make mistakes; a mother who had no use for two girls who used her bathroom and ate her food.

Last spring when the terrible thing happened, Sarah had begun to dream that her real mother lived in another town somewhere and would come to get her some day. It even seemed possible, given that Sarah didn't look much like the rest of the Nevilles, with her light brown, almost blond hair. Although Dad's hair was now thin and gray, Carlie and her mother both had dark hair. Sarah had seen pictures of the two of them together in the hospital, Carlie in a little pink cap and Mother in her satin bed jacket.

Maybe there were similar pictures of Sarah in boxes somewhere, but she had never seen them, and that's where the daydream always stopped. She couldn't bear to think that she and Carlie weren't sisters after all.

Their mother was "nervous," Dad had said once, but he didn't seem worried about it, and Sarah suspected he didn't want to think about such things. When the two of them went dancing, she seemed happy, so maybe that was enough for him.

Sarah turned toward her sister's bed. "Carlie, you asleep already?" She blew her nose loudly. The loneliest time in the world came after Carlie had drifted off, and Sarah was left to listen to the tiny particles of darkness bump into each other.

"Hey," she whispered, "wanna play Draw-in-the-Dark?"

Carlie stirred. "Mm, not tonight. . . ."

"Please. Just one round? We haven't played all week."

"Oh, Sarah. . . ." Covers rustled and Carlie rose up on one elbow.

That meant yes. Smiling in the darkness, Sarah leaned over the edge of her bed to pull out the tablet and pencil she kept for their games. She tore off a sheet of paper and handed it across the space to Carlie. Then she took one for herself and folded it into four squares while Carlie folded hers. Usually, they played several rounds, filling the paper with four different pictures. But one was better than nothing.

"You go first," Sarah whispered.

Carlie sighed. "Okay . . . Bride gowns. The ones we're going to wear someday?"

Sarah laughed quietly. "That's easy." Feeling for the upper left-hand square, she filled the top with a round head and fluffy veil. Then she made little circles for the eyes and mouth, guessing where they should go.

It was mostly Carlie who wanted to get married someday, but Sarah played along, adding spiky daisies and a long gown flowing into the next square. They would laugh at the disjointed pictures in the morning.

"I know, let's have some more raisins," Sarah suggested. "We can pretend it's popcorn and we're in a movie theater."

"It's *not* popcorn, and we have to be careful. There aren't that many left."

"Just a few, I promise." Sarah hurried across the cold floor to the cupboard, ducking under the low part of the ceiling. Kneeling in front of the hole, she pried open the panel and reached in; her fingers closed around a napkin holding some little lumps.

"Got 'em. . . ." Sarah sprang up. *Rrrip!* Her toe caught in the hem of her nightgown and she fell sidewise onto the cold floor.

"Shh!" Carlie hissed.

The napkin flew out of Sarah's hand. At the same time, the wall panel fell with a dull thump. Carlie gasped.

The entire house seemed to draw in its breath. Then downstairs, their mother's ceramic ashtray clanked onto the coffee table. Slippered feet marched through the house for the second time.

Frantically, Sarah swept the floor with her arm, trying to find the raisins before their mother made it up the stairs.

"Under the bed!" Carlie breathed. In the dim light, she lifted up the quilt just long enough for Sarah to brush the raisins underneath.

Sarah's heart pounded with familiar dread as she flew onto her bed. Why had she broken the stay-in-bed rule when she knew what could happen?

Again the door twanged open. Light from the kitchen flooded the stairwell. Quick footsteps hit the stairs. Sarah stiffened as her mother's silhouette rose up out of the stairwell like a black ghost. Then the bedroom lights came on bright, and Carlie and Sarah squinted at each other in horror.

Their mother strode all the way into their tiny room, filling it up as if she were a big child trying to fit herself into a doll's house. With her had come the scent of violet bath salts that followed her everywhere. As she stopped between the two beds, the silky rosebud robe settled like curtains around her legs.

"What are you doing to me?" Sharp, arched eyebrows pulled together in a furious scowl. A thin slice of mouth twitched as if with the effort of finding the right word. "*Defiant*, that's what you are. I expect to be obeyed when I tell you to go to sleep. Didn't I tell you to go to sleep?"

Sarah tried not to look at the strap tied at their mother's waist, but she stared at it, wincing, willing it to stay in its place.

"I asked you a question!" their mother snarled, giving the strap an angry yank.

Then moving only her eyes, she fixed her scowl on Carlie. Little lines puckered inward around her mouth as if the years and years of smoking had simply stuck there.

"Answer me!"

"Yes," Carlie said coolly.

"Yes, what!" she demanded, her eyes narrowing.

Sarah flashed to Carlie, whose lips were set in a tight line. Their mother wanted her sister to repeat the whole thing: *Yes, Mama, you told us to go to sleep*. But Sarah knew Carlie wouldn't say it no matter what.

"ANSWER ME!" White fingers clutched at the bathrobe strap.

In desperation, Sarah stared at Carlie, hoping she could somehow reach into her sister's thoughts. *Just say it so she'll go back downstairs*. But the words spilled from her own mouth. "Yes, you told us to go to sleep."

"Shut up, you little fool; I'm not talking to you."

Sarah flinched like she always did when sharp words were aimed directly at her.

The rosebud sleeves folded over their mother's chest, and a painful silence followed. Finally turning away from Sarah, she looked down at the floor where a single black raisin lay barely an inch from her slipper. Then her eyes moved toward the wall.

Sarah could not stop her hand from clapping over her mouth. In that moment, she forgot about her sore throat and runny nose and instead thought only about the next two minutes. Something terrible was going to happen. The cupboard lay exposed like a great mouth caught midscream.

two

SARAH'S MIND SNAPPED back to one night last spring. It had been raining for three days straight, and the whole world looked soggy and gray. Dad was still at work while their mother sat in the kitchen, smoking cigarette after cigarette. The tobacco smell came right up through the vent into Sarah and Carlie's room. They had already washed their faces and gotten ready for bed, but they were sitting at the top of the stairs together, listening for the sounds of dinner—pans, silverware, the refrigerator opening.

Finally, their mother got up, but not to cook a meal. Instead, her footsteps went into the bathroom.

"She's not fixing us anything," Sarah whispered. "I told you so."

Then without warning, "Get down here, both of you!" In a flash their mother was at the bottom of the stairs, yanking open the old wooden door.

The girls hurried down to stand before her in the kitchen. What could they have done this time? Then Sarah noticed the towel, the same embroidered towel she had seen earlier hanging on the hook next to the bathroom sink. It had been brand new and clean then, but now there was a dirty smudge on one end.

"Which one of you *filthy* things did this?" The way she said it, the word itself might have contained a contagious slime. She flung the towel into the sink.

"I guess I used it," Carlie admitted. "I had soap in my eyes. . . ."

"You snit. You did this to me on purpose." Their mother glowered as she clutched at the strap on her robe. "I won't have it! *I won't!*" Her voice grew louder. Carlie backed up against the wall. Then she slid her bathrobe strap out of its loops. The silky fabric seemed almost to flutter before she grabbed it in both hands and jerked it taut.

What in the world was she doing? Sarah's heart pounded as she watched her mother loop the strap twice around her left hand. She had hit them plenty of times—she had even knocked Carlie down more than once—but she'd never done anything really brutal. Words screamed inside Sarah's head, yet no sound would come, not even when her mother lunged at Carlie and pinned her by the neck against the kitchen wall.

"Don't you ever . . . I've told you . . . don't you

19

ever touch my things!" Gritting her teeth, she pushed harder and harder, the strip of flowered cloth cutting into Carlie's neck.

Carlie clawed at the strap, shocked, pop-eyed. Sarah did not want to look at her sister's purple face, but she was too mesmerized to turn away. It even occurred to her, almost calmly, that this was what murder looked like, and that it was happening right in front of her.

Finally, the strap fell. Had her mother simply gone back into her room after that? Sarah couldn't remember. She had merely stood by while Carlie sucked in great lungfuls of air, struggled to keep her balance, then held on to the wall as she stood gasping in the stairwell. She made her way back up the stairs, crying and rubbing her throat.

Sarah managed to follow close behind, ready to catch her if she fell. Then at the top of the stairs, Carlie had turned toward her with a look so alone it had torn at Sarah's heart. She had done nothing to help her sister, nothing at all. Even now, the realization made her squirm with shame. She should have kicked her mother, or something, but she had not.

Later when Dad got home, their parents took up their usual places in the living room and listened to President Eisenhower on the radio. Nothing had been said about the girls or what had happened at the bottom of the stairs.

Sarah gagged at the very memory of that day, the

day she had found out that their mother really could do unspeakable things, and that there was no one to help them. That was the day, too, when Sarah and Carlie had made a secret pledge never to call her Mama again.

Now Sarah looked into that same angry face, the eyes now focused on a raisin on the floor. Their mother stood for a moment as if she expected it to crawl away, then touched the black spot with the toe of her slipper and stooped to pick it up.

"What's this?" She poked at the raisin in the palm of her hand.

Neither girl answered. They watched their mother pinch the raisin between her fingers, then cut it in half with her thumbnail and raise a piece to her nostrils. She sniffed it several times with a puzzled look on her face. Then she turned slowly, sweeping the floor with her eyes. When her gaze reached the foot of Carlie's bed, her head jerked back.

Sarah's hand went to her neck.

"So!" Her robe billowing, their mother flew to the dark space of the cupboard.

The board just fell out somehow. Sarah's mind raced to find an excuse and she glanced at Carlie, but her sister's eyes stayed riveted on the back of their mother's head. A rosebud-covered arm extended into the hole and came back out with a limp paper bag.

Their mother held it away from her as the

21

bottom of the bag tore open. A square of oily orange cheese hit the floor. "Oooh!" she howled. "This is . . . it's *sick*!"

Next, their mother pulled napkins and bags of bread crusts, cherry pits and withered carrots out of the space under the eaves.

Sarah's face burned with humiliation.

The last to come out was the rest of the bread Carlie had stashed half an hour earlier. Their mother dumped each parcel on the floor and flicked at the contents with one finger. Finally, she stood up and pulled her robe back into place.

"You're stealing food . . . that's what this is. You've been sneaking down into my kitchen."

Sarah looked over at Carlie, silently pleading for her to save them, but Carlie did not move or even blink.

"You filthy things. How can you live like this?" Their mother shuddered dramatically, then dashed to the head of the stairs. "Hal? Hal, come here."

Downstairs their father's chair creaked. If she were angry, he'd have to be angry, too. He was fourteen years older, but he always acted however she wanted him to.

"Get this trash out of here," their mother ordered, returning to the center of the room. "You want rats up here living with you? Serve you right."

Sarah looked down at her own hands clutching the blankets. She had never seen their cupboard as something dirty, only as a necessity. Maybe it *was* sick.

"Tt!"

When their father ascended into the room, he looked down at the mound of garbage on the floor in disbelief. "What's all this?" he asked. His round face, naturally red, registered more embarrassment than anger, as if anything having to do with the girls was beyond him.

Sarah gulped. How could she possibly explain? "We got hungry," she said at last.

"That's ridiculous," their mother countered.

"Hungry? Didn't you get enough dinner?" their father asked.

There wasn't any dinner. Sarah didn't dare say it. Dad wouldn't believe them anyway, and then they'd be in worse trouble for telling on their mother. She looked into his pale eyes, wishing he could figure it out for himself, but he had already formed another thought.

"Please clean it up," he said, "and don't be doing this again. I want you girls to stop upsetting your mom." Assignment completed, he scuffed his way back down the stairs.

"Tt! You heard your father."

Sarah refused to look into her mother's eyes. She could tell she liked this, seeing them in trouble with Dad.

"Fine thanks I get for being a mother," she

wound up. "Just wait, you'll see what it's like. Never a possession or a thought to yourself. Never a moment's peace. Well, I'm not about to let you two ruin my health." Then with a final yank to her bathrobe strap, she left them to their chore.

Without looking at each other, the girls got out of bed and knelt in front of their cupboard. They had heard similar speeches before. But now a new feeling of shame crept down Sarah's back. She hadn't thought of rats. There could be one in here this very minute, waiting to bite her fingers.

Now stealing food seemed like a terrible thing to do, hungry or not. What if the kids at school found out she and her sister did such things? She would never be able to face them again.

After a few minutes of reaching carefully into the cupboard and bringing out the last wads of paper and stale foods, Sarah and Carlie turned toward each other. It was over.

Carlie's lips pulled into a tight line. "We'll find another place," she said in a low voice. "This time we'll find a way to get rid of the garbage."

"No, Carlie. I don't want to do it anymore." Sarah felt an intense desire to be clean, to wash her clothes and take a bath.

"It'll be okay," Carlie promised. "This is her fault, not ours. We have to eat, don't we?"

"I don't know." Sarah stuffed all the small bags into a long Wonder Bread bag. When everything was out of the cupboard, she and Carlie fit the wallboard back into place. The music for *Our Miss Brooks* bounced up through the vent, but Sarah had no interest in listening.

For a long time, she stared at the squares in the ceiling and thought about rats.

The next morning, Carlie got out of bed and looked out the back window. "Dad's already gone." She rocked from one foot to the other. "Just great. I really need to go to the bathroom."

"Everyone wants their floors waxed on Saturday," Sarah said. She needed to use the bathroom, too, but the rule was they couldn't make noise by flushing the toilet, not until she'd had her coffee and a cigarette and had called them downstairs. Better to think about something else.

"Hey, my throat's not sore anymore," Sarah announced, testing it with a swallow. "It just tickles this morning. . . ."

Carlie didn't seem to hear her. "Listen!" Downstairs their mother coughed, then water ran and the furnace moaned.

Sarah crept to the head of the stairs to stand beside Carlie. She heard the refrigerator open. "Maybe we'll get some breakfast," she whispered, though she knew that could be hours. Peering out the narrow window into the backyard, Sarah took in the brilliance of the blue October sky behind the

25

leaves of the apple tree.

"Look," she said pointing down into the yard. "It's not stealing if we pick up some of those apples. The tree makes apples for everyone."

"Lot of good it does us," Carlie complained. "We're stuck in here."

"Maybe not." Sarah felt suddenly energized. "I have a library book to return. If we don't return it, there'll be a fine."

"You're right, and there's a bathroom in the library!" Now Carlie smiled.

Both girls dressed quickly. So far, their mother had no rule about the library. It was the one escape allowed to them, though after last night she might be in a different mood.

Carlie slid a folded paper bag into the back of her blue pants and pulled her shirt down over the bulge.

They moved boldly down the stairs and crossed the speckled linoleum of the kitchen floor. Sarah poked her head around the doorway to the living room. Their mother sat slumped on the couch facing the piano, wrapped in her pink rosebuds. A ribbon of smoke curled from the cigarette in her left hand.

"We have to go to the library," Sarah said. "I have a book almost overdue." "Almost overdue" sounded more urgent than just "due."

When their mother didn't answer or acknowledge them, the girls hurried toward the back door.

They crossed the porch in two strides.

"Carlisle! Sarah!" The sound came from the living room—she hadn't bothered to get off the couch.

"I said, we have to go to the library," Sarah called. She grabbed Carlie's arm and the two ran across the backyard. Along the back side of the garage was the alley with weeds and hollyhocks growing around two dented garbage cans.

"You open the door and get the bikes," Carlie ordered. "I'll get us some apples."

Sarah wrestled one of the garage doors open and wheeled her blue bicycle out into the gravel driveway. The broken carrier on the back flopped noisily. Carlie's bike was an old red Schwinn with a bar across the middle, a boys' bike. Sarah propped it outside and closed the door. She straddled her own bike with one foot on the pedal, ready to take off.

Sarah glanced across the alley to the gas station, where a boy in coveralls stood watching them. She knew there was a bathroom on the far side, and they had used it a few times, but there was no way she would go over there with someone watching. Sarah looked away.

Carlie appeared, hugging a heavy-looking paper bag. "Here." Little yellow apples thumped into the wire basket on the front of Sarah's bike.

"Oh, brother, I *really* have to go to the bathroom," Carlie said, and she looked toward the gas station. When she noticed the boy, she blushed. He waved.

"Do you know him?" Sarah asked.

"Sort of. Come on, let's go."

Sarah pushed hard on her pedal and rolled out of the driveway. She didn't look back until they had turned onto Thirty-seventh Street. From this distance their house looked saggy and gray, with huge trees hiding their bedroom windows. Dad had said they were lucky to be on a corner, but just one block away was Grand, the busy street of grocery stores and other businesses that led from South Hill to downtown Spokane. Their street, Sherman, was lined with small shingled houses where overgrown lilac bushes hung over picket fences.

Sarah took in a deep breath of freedom and looked over at her sister pumping her bike furiously. She maneuvered close to Carlie and handed her an apple. Her sister's hair was flying like a flag behind her in the cool autumn air.

They reached the stone building and pushed their bikes into the stands.

"We made it," Carlie said. "The good ol' library." She dashed up the walk ahead of Sarah, who finished her apple and threw the core into the bushes.

Sarah caught up with her. "Hey, I'm pretty smart, aren't I, Carlie?"

"You're a genius." Carlie smiled over her

shoulder without slowing her pace.

The girls went straight to the women's restroom, then Sarah slipped her book onto the return pile at the front desk. It wasn't actually due for another week, but she had read it in two nights, right after checking it out.

The library was mostly one large room with rows of bookshelves and a smaller room where two librarians pasted and taped damaged books. In the back, by the history section, were two tiny restrooms and a drinking fountain. What Sarah loved most about the library, though, was a window right in the ceiling where the sun shone down on four upholstered chairs facing one another in a square.

From the tall shelves, Carlie picked a book by Emily Loring, her favorite author. On the cover were a pretty girl and a boy leaning over her shoulder. Sarah checked out a science fiction book with a silver space station on the cover.

The girls each claimed one of the chairs and started reading. Sarah looked up more than once at the people moving around, people with sisters and brothers and parents, people whose stories she would never know. They all looked normal, not like her and Carlie.

She started to sniff again, but only a little. *An apple a day keeps the doctor away.* Sarah had eaten six so far. Every few minutes, she checked the light in the glass square above them as time stretched into delicious hours. Finally, with the sky a deep blue, she pointed upward and sighed. "It's getting dark."

"So what? We're already in trouble," Carlie said, but they got up and made a last stop at the restroom and the drinking fountain.

"Maybe she's in a better mood by now." Sarah swiped the back of her hand across her chin.

"I doubt it."

"I'm getting hungry for mashed potatoes and pork chops and hot rolls."

"Stop it," Carlie said. "Just don't think about it. We'll get something to eat somehow." She hurried out the door and loped down the stairs. Sarah ran after her.

In a moment they were on their bikes, whizzing home through neighborhoods of brick, then wooden houses. When they turned onto Sherman again, Sarah looked down the street to their house, where Dad's green panel truck sat in the driveway.

"Good, he's home," Carlie said. "I hope he hasn't already eaten."

"Maybe we'll get lucky." If there were no dinner for them again, he might let them make sandwiches or something.

They pedaled harder the last half block, Sarah's stomach gurgling uncomfortably. At home they put their bikes away, gathered their books and tiptoed in through the screened back porch.

Upon entering the kitchen, Sarah nearly fell

against the wall with the unmistakable aroma of fried chicken. There on the kitchen counter were two flat boxes with pictures of the contents: corn, potatoes, three pieces of chicken.

"TV dinners," Sarah whispered. "They must be in the oven." She'd seen them advertised, but their mother had said she'd never buy anything so silly.

"Only two." Carlie moaned.

On the other side of the kitchen, the bathroom door stood ajar and water ran in the footed bathtub. Mounds of bubbles threatened to spill over onto the floor.

Laughter and talking suddenly came from the bedroom beyond. In a fit of giggles, their mother dashed into the bathroom and turned off the water. Sarah jumped back from the counter.

When she saw the girls, she smiled. "There you are. Your father and I are going out—dinner and dancing." She let out a happy sigh as if last night and this morning hadn't happened at all.

"Oh." Sarah glanced toward the stove, where she could almost see through the solid oven door to the little metal trays of food, for them.

"We thought we'd leave you girls here by yourselves this time. You're old enough to handle that, aren't you?"

"Well . . . sure." Of course they were old enough, Sarah thought. What their mother meant was, could she trust them to follow her rules?

Carlie's eyes were open wide, and Sarah knew she and her sister were thinking the same thoughts: They would be alone to get into the refrigerator. Alone to turn on the television and change the channels. Alone to use the bathroom whenever they wanted. But most of all, they would be able to devour every bit of the wonderful food they smelled.

Their parents went out from time to time, but in the past, Josephine had always come over, and the girls were given instructions to stay upstairs and not bother her. They always bothered her anyway, because Josephine liked them, but this would be entirely different.

Sarah touched her stomach, tight and sore from eating so many apples. A whole evening alone. Just the two of them.

three

"AND, CARLIE, BE sure to take out the garbage."
The girls' mother chattered as she looked over her
shoulder into the full-length mirror on the bathroom
door. In the back of her black dress, at her waist, a
giant satin bow caught layers and layers of crinkly
skirts. Dad stood by in his gray slacks, grinning at
her.

"Did you hear me, honey?"

"Yes," Carlie answered.

Their mother fluffed her skirts and sucked on her
cigarette. "The number for the Elks Club is on the
pad next to the phone," she said. Her face was
flushed a bright peach color, as it always was when
she and Dad went dancing.

Sarah wished they'd just leave. Their mother had
been getting ready for the past hour, while their dinner sat covered on top of the stove. She had not
given them permission to go ahead and eat, and
rules from long ago told them it was not okay to ask.

Instead, the girls stayed downstairs to wash the day's coffee cups and saucers while the smells of violets, fried chicken, and cigarette smoke mingled together in one chaotic aroma.

Finally, Dad put on his overcoat and they said good-bye.

Sarah and Carlie watched through the window in the back door as the headlights pulled away from the garage, then turned left and moved away down Grand.

"They're gone!" Sarah stood motionless for a moment, taking in the open feel of the house. Then a sudden fit of joy sent her flying to the stove. She worked the foil off the top of one of the TV dinners and pushed the other tray toward Carlie. There in the little metal sections were three pieces of crispy chicken, a flattened mound of mashed potatoes and lovely, yellow corn.

They both stood at the stove and tore into their first piece of chicken.

"Mmm," Sarah murmured.

Carlie found a bottle of milk in the refrigerator and guzzled half of it before she stopped to catch her breath. "Come on, let's eat the rest of this in front of the TV."

"We can use their coffee table." With a blissful tingle crawling from Sarah's toes to her scalp, she danced into the living room, where she played with the knobs on the television until she found the one that turned on the big console.

On the screen, two gray faces were stuck together in a kiss. "Oh, boy," Carlie said. "This is going to be great."

Sarah set her tray and a glass of milk on the coffee table, and the girls perched side by side on the couch.

"It tastes so good," Sarah repeated between forkfuls. Though the potatoes were only lukewarm now, they were wonderfully thick and salty, just as Sarah had imagined. When she swallowed, the food seemed almost to drop to the bottom of her stomach and bounce before settling.

While Carlie stared at the monotonous, romantic scenes on the television, Sarah busied herself looking around the wallpapered room. They didn't get to come in here often, even though the living room always seemed like the most important part of the house.

Next to a little writing desk in the corner hung a framed photograph of their parents before they were married. Their mother was leaning against an old-fashioned car with a cigarette in her hand. Her black hair was blowing in the wind, and she was squinting into the sun. She looked just like a movie star, Sarah thought. Dad's head was tilted toward her with an adoring look on his face. He had seemed old even then, with a bent nose and a thin wisp of hair hanging over his forehead.

On the far side of the room stood the piano, so shiny Sarah could see her face in the wood of the high back. A small bust of someone famous sat on top. A wooden metronome sat there, too. One time her mother had let Sarah open the little door and set the hand ticking, but that had been a long time ago. The piano lid was closed over the keys now, and the bench was pushed all the way in.

The music grew louder on the television, and the program ended. Sarah turned to Carlie, smiling. "Okay, what should we do next?"

"I know what I want to do," Carlie said. "I want to take a bath."

Sarah could still smell her mother's violets coming from the bathroom. "Me, too. Do you think we have time?"

"They probably haven't even had dinner yet," Carlie answered, "but we can get in together if you want. I'll take out the garbage. You start the dishes."

They cleared the coffee table and replaced the basket of matchbooks that always sat in the middle. Then they dropped the metal trays into the brown paper bag under the sink.

Carlie ran upstairs and came back with the garbage from last night. She hoisted both bags into her arms.

"Want me to come with you?" Sarah offered. "I could hold a flashlight."

"No, I can manage," Carlie said. She went out

the back door, letting the screen door bump shut behind her.

Sarah submerged forks and glasses into the water in the sink. Even doing these few dishes alone with Carlie was going to be fun. This is the best night ever, she thought, and she felt her mouth pull into a smile all by itself. Her reflection in the darkened window above the sink smiled back.

Sarah studied herself, deciding that tonight she looked almost pretty. She experimented with her mouth, parting her lips and grinning at herself, showing all of her teeth. Then, suddenly feeling foolish, she let her face sag into its normal expression and refocused on the dishes in the sink.

Sarah washed each piece of silverware and the glasses, rinsed them off and set them upright in the drainer for Carlie to dry. She glanced toward the back door, at the window that reflected back another picture of herself. This picture looked annoyed. Carlie was taking a long time with the garbage.

Sarah pushed the salt and pepper shakers into place, then went to the back door and peered out. What could be taking so long? She pictured the garbage cans out in the alley behind the garage. It could be scary out there in the dark, she thought.

She moved to the porch and opened the screen door, hoping to see Carlie's shadow coming along the walk. But there was no sign of her.

"Carlie?" Sarah called in a tone just above a

whisper. Little splats of rain had begun to hit the sidewalk.

Sarah closed the door and stepped back into the kitchen. Could Carlie be playing a joke on her? Maybe she was outside sitting on the fence, watching Sarah smile at herself in the glass. Sarah whirled toward the window and stuck out her tongue. "So there!" she said out loud. "That's what you get for making me do the dishes by myself."

Feeling watched now, Sarah set to work tidying the kitchen as if she were acting for a movie. When she finished and had hung up the wet dish towel, she watched herself fold her arms with a jerk. "Come on, Carlie," she said. "It's no fun being in the house all by yourself."

Where could Carlie have gone? It took only a minute or two to take out the garbage. How could she leave Sarah alone on a special night like this? Unless something had happened to her.

Sarah stood staring at the door, wondering what to do. Then she took the silver flashlight out of the kitchen drawer. She lifted her coat off the hook by the back door, put it on and flipped the hood up over her head. Through the open screen door, she slowly swept the yard with the flashlight.

"Carlie? You out there?" A breeze rattled the trees, and raindrops came more steadily now. Even if Carlie answered, Sarah might not hear her.

"Carlie?" Sarah's heart pounded as she

approached the alley side of the garage. What would she find? Without knowing why she did it, she turned off the flashlight.

Sarah took another step, then stopped, frozen. Carlie's head and shoulders and long dark hair were silhouetted against the lights from the gas station. A boy was standing with her, and they were talking. The boy laughed and then Carlie laughed. Sarah saw his hand reach up and touch Carlie's shoulder.

Sarah gasped. It must be that boy who works there, she thought, the one who saw them leave on their bikes. Why hadn't Carlie told her about this? She whirled around and ran toward the light in the kitchen, taking all three porch steps in one stride. Back in the kitchen, an ugly feeling expanded inside her until she thought she would choke on it.

A minute later, Carlie came in, too. "Were you just outside?" Carlie asked.

"No," Sarah said. She could not look at her sister. "As you can see, I was cleaning up the kitchen."

"Sorry."

Sarah turned around, feeling her lip quiver. Carlie's face seemed almost to be glowing, like her mother's whenever she went dancing. "Where were you? I did the dishes all by myself."

"I was just talking to Jesse. He works at the gas station. Is that a crime? Besides, there were only forks and glasses."

"So?" Sarah looked at the floor. Carlie had said

she knew that boy *sort of.* How could she have kept a secret like this from Sarah? For an instant, she wondered if Carlie had ever kissed him. Then she blinked, making the thought go away.

"Come on," Carlie said. "You still want to take a bath, don't you?"

"I don't know."

"Sure you do. Come on. Who knows when we'll be able to again." Carlie waited, then said, "Well, I'm taking a bath. You can get in if you want to or take one later," and she went into the bathroom and started the water in the tub.

Sarah stood in the kitchen, fighting back tears. She felt as if her life were ending or that she would never again be happy. She and Carlie didn't need anyone crowding between them. Sarah had believed her sister felt the same way.

Carlie hummed in her wispy voice while water filled the tub, creating a cloud of steam. She was running it nice and hot.

Sarah moved slowly to the door to watch. "You'd better not use any of her bubble bath," she said. "She'll notice."

"And we'll smell like violets," Carlie answered with a laugh.

Sarah pulled off her shoes without untying them. If she stayed mad at Carlie, their special night would be over.

Carlie smiled like herself again, and Sarah forced

herself to smile back. "I know," she suggested, feeling better, "I'll turn off all the lights except here in the bathroom. If they come home early, the house will look dark. We'll have time to run upstairs."

"Okay, hurry."

With a growing sense of excitement, Sarah ran through the house turning off lights, then got two faded beach towels and set them on the toilet cover. "We can let these dry upstairs, then put them away later. No one will ever know."

Steam billowed up in the tiny bathroom and swirled around the lightbulb in the ceiling. It dampened the fancy glass bottles on the narrow shelf above the tub.

Sarah opened the mirrored door to their parents' bedroom and peeked in. Another of her mother's rules was that they not go in there, and she felt guilty now for looking. A high bed filled most of the room. Against a polished wooden headboard rested four pillows in embroidered cases. Carved pineapples topped four enormously tall, slender bedposts.

Carlie dropped her shirt on the bathroom floor. Sarah pulled the door between the bedroom and the bathroom shut and took her clothes off, too. She climbed quickly into the tub, letting the hot water flow around her and fill in all the spaces as she sat down. "Ooh!" she gasped. "It feels so good. Come on, Carlie. Get in."

"I'm coming." Carlie lowered herself slowly into

the water. "Ooh."

The girls sat facing each other, smiling, dipping their arms and shoulders into the water. Sarah pushed her legs down flat, bumping into Carlie's feet, relishing the hot sting on her knees.

"When I get married," Carlie mused, "everyone's going to have their own bathroom, even the kids. One for every bedroom."

"Gee, that would be a mansion. Let's draw bathrooms in the dark tonight," Sarah suggested. "I already know what mine will look like."

"Not until we make a new cupboard," Carlie said. "I don't want to eat apples for breakfast and lunch again."

Sarah sat in silence, swishing her hands through the water. For the first time ever, she couldn't think of anything to say to her sister. She was thinking about apples and that boy at the gas station.

Carlie looked up, her face beaded from the steam. "Jesse is really nice," she said, as if she were reading Sarah's mind. "He's not like the boys at school."

"What do you mean?"

"Jesse understands things."

"Things like what?"

"Things about us."

Sarah felt her face go hot. "Not . . . you don't mean, about the cupboard and everything! What did you tell him?"

"Don't worry," Carlie said. "I didn't tell any real secrets. Just some things about her."

"Oh," Sarah said. Still, she wondered how Carlie could stand out by the garbage cans and talk about such personal things to a boy. It was embarrassing. And now he knew about Sarah, too.

"Well, where does he live? Where does he go to school?"

"Jesse doesn't live anywhere exactly," Carlie said.

The telephone rang in the kitchen and the girls looked at each other.

"Should we answer it?" Sarah asked. No one ever called them. "It's probably about waxing floors."

The phone rang a second time and a third. Carlie rose up out of the tub, wrapped a towel around herself and ran out of the bathroom. A trail of little puddles followed her.

"Hello?"

Sarah sat still in the tub and listened.

"Fine. Oh, we're just . . . you know . . . talking."

Their parents. Sarah felt exposed now, and she pushed the bathroom door closed except for a small crack where she could listen.

Carlie ran back into the bathroom. "They're going to be home in a little while," she said. "That could mean a few minutes. Come on, let's hurry."

Sarah's heart lurched, and she pulled the plug in

the tub. "You said they haven't even eaten." She stepped out onto the wet floor and unfolded her towel.

"A little while. That's what Dad said."

Now everything looked wet, even the walls, the windowsill and the fringed, vinyl shade. Sarah dried off, then dropped her towel on the floor and scooted it around the bathroom under her bare feet. She dried every surface she could reach. Carlie wiped the steam off the mirror.

Sarah wondered if other kids worried so much about everything—she didn't think so. It was just at their house, where their mother didn't want them around, that girls had to be invisible.

When they were finished, they dashed upstairs.

"Okay," Carlie said. "We've got to find a loose square for our new cupboard." She felt around the walls, tapping as she went.

"We don't have time," Sarah protested.

"Yes, we do—hurry."

"But what about the rats?" Sarah asked.

"There aren't any rats," Carlie assured her. "We would have seen them by now. She just said that to scare us."

Sarah guessed that was true. She jumped on her bed and felt along one of the seams. Inserting her fingernail along a crack, she pried at the wall panel. In a moment, she had lifted it out. "Look, Carlie. It came out real easy."

Both girls peered into the dark space. The hole did not seem to go back as far as the first cupboard, and it dropped down two feet or more. Bits of wood and a bent nail lay at the bottom.

"Maybe we could put a cardboard box in here, like a table," Carlie suggested.

The girls ran to the back porch for an empty cardboard box. There were several stacked inside each other that had once carried Dad's supplies. When the table had been folded down to size and set up, they went back down into the kitchen with the teapot from their doll dishes and opened one cupboard after another. Sarah listened for the crunch of Dad's truck on the gravel outside.

They found a box of pretzels, packages of cherry Kool-Aid, some chewing gum, a half bag of potato chips, some dry noodles, a box of saltines, more raisins and an old thermos bottle. They filled the thermos with water and the teapot with sugar, then took some of everything they had gathered.

Sarah filled a paper bag with pretzels, closed the box and turned it upside down to fluff the remaining pretzels so the box would look full again.

When they returned upstairs, they arranged their stash on top of the cardboard box.

"I won't even have to get out of bed to get into this cupboard," Sarah pointed out. She stood in the middle of the room, contemplating what they'd done. If a second cupboard were found, they'd be in a lot more trouble than the first time. But now they had food, lots of it. As a last measure, she propped up her old doll Rosemary and a stuffed puppy named Otto in front of the square.

"It'll be a secret forever," Sarah pledged. "We aren't going to tell anyone, right, Carlie?"

"Right," Carlie said.

Sarah searched her sister's face to see if anything more were written there. When she saw nothing except the usual Carlie, she smiled, trying to ignore the uneasy question that had crept into her thoughts: she and Carlie were going to stick together always, weren't they?

four

SARAH AND CARLIE put on their nightgowns and sat on their beds, facing each other. Sarah wished she had a clean, pretty one to wear, one without a torn hem, but at least she'd had a bath. Her sister hadn't mentioned that boy again.

Sarah got up and flipped off the light, then knelt on her bed. "They won't ask any questions if they think we're asleep." She moved Rosemary and Otto out of the way and pried open the panel. "Want some pretzels?"

"Sure."

"Coming right up." Sarah parceled some out for Carlie and took a handful for herself. The familiar feeling of safety and comfort wrapped around her like a fuzzy blanket, as it always did when they had a full cupboard. As long as she had Carlie and some-thing to eat, almost everything she needed was right here in this room.

"I wish they'd go dancing every night, don't

47

you?" Sarah nibbled the salt off her pretzel and fit the panel back into place.

"She's going to be in a good mood tomorrow."

In truth, Sarah wished their parents wouldn't come home at all. Pictures strolled through her mind as she snuggled down under her covers. Their mother and father had suddenly left for Kentucky, and she and Carlie lived in the house alone. The girls cooked dinner, went off to school together and invited friends over.

Sarah saw herself and Carlie moving around the house, going into every room. They played tunes on the piano. They divided their mother's pretty dresses and shared the shoes and earrings. Sarah lay gazing through the tree outside their window, feeling her heart beat with the possibilities.

A long time later, the moon had risen and was shining directly in the window on Sarah's face. Her parents still were not home. Dad had said hours ago that they'd be home in a little while. Now she felt worried. What if Dad's truck had gotten hit by the train whistling through town? If they really didn't come home now, it might be her fault for wishing it.

Sarah lay in bed, feeling alone and guilty. She heard a car turn at the corner and continue down the street. Someone pulled out of a driveway; the headlights cast a yellow-blue arc on the ceiling, then rolled away. She listened to a distant siren, and wondered if it were an ambulance heading for the train tracks. It occurred to her to go downstairs and check the time, but the kitchen seemed unfriendly and off-limits again.

By the time Dad's truck finally made its familiar sound in the gravel driveway, Sarah's ears felt almost stretched. The truck door slammed. A moment later, the back door opened and they came into the house laughing.

Sarah sat up on her elbows. Doors opened on each side of the bathroom, one after the other. She listened to shoes dropping, water running in the bathroom sink and her mother giggling again. If they noticed that the girls had taken a bath, they weren't saying anything.

Finally, Sarah dropped back down onto her pillow and went to sleep.

The next sounds she heard were of pans clanking in the kitchen. The sun streamed in through the window, and a wonderful smell drifted up from downstairs.

Carlie was already sitting up in bed drawing pictures, as if she'd been waiting for Sarah to wake up.

"I told you she'd be in a good mood today," Carlie said. "She's fixing breakfast—waffles and bacon."

Sarah sat up and turned her nose toward the stairwell.

"Girls?" It was their mother at the bottom of the stairs. "Come on down."

Sarah shot a smile at Carlie. "Coming." They threw back their covers, put on slippers and bathrobes and hurried down the stairs.

Still wearing her makeup from the night before, their mother was pouring thick yellow batter onto the waffle iron. *Psst!* it hissed when she lowered the lid. Dad sat at the kitchen table with the Sunday paper, and Sarah noticed a soft, peaceful look on his face.

It was clear that they would all be eating together at the same table this morning, instead of their parents eating alone in the dining room like they usually did.

When they were all seated with breakfast in front of them, their mother started talking excitedly. "Well . . ." The word slid out in a happy gust as if she were releasing balloons into the sky.

"You girls should have been there," she said, her eyes shining. "We asked Eugene to play 'Stardust,' and everyone moved out of our way so we could dance. We cleared the floor."

Sarah imagined her mother twirling round and round while everyone else sat at little tables and watched.

Dad grinned, and their mother's voice swept on as if she were still dancing. "I always said I wanted to do exhibition dancing. Lanny has been begging me to take lessons and get into dance competitions."

Lanny was a dance instructor who seemed to be at the Elks Club whenever their parents went there.

"You don't want to do that," Dad said through a mouthful. "Those people are up all hours of the night, getting on buses and bedding down in strange hotel rooms."

Their mother frowned. "I'm only saying he thinks I should, Hal." She got up and put more batter in the waffle iron. "Daddy always said I was a natural. I can still remember when the folks picked me and Janey up from the school dances."

She sat down again, reached for her cigarette and stared out the window as if she could see it all again. "On the way home, he'd tell Mom, 'Janey turns heads . . .'"

Sarah finished the sentence in her mind. *Janey turns heads, but it's Margaret who's the dancer.*

The look on their mother's face was one of deep seriousness, as if her daddy was never wrong and it was still just a matter of time before it all came true.

Dad reached over and patted their mother's hand. "And I'm the one who got her," he said, looking a little shy.

"Yeah, well, maybe," their mother answered. Like she always did.

The corner of Carlie's mouth pulled up into the slightest smile, as if she understood secret things about love.

Sarah squirmed, remembering last night. "Tell us

about your house," she said, changing the subject. This was her favorite story. She reached for another strip of bacon.

Their mother pushed her chair back and crossed her legs, arranging her flowered robe over her knee. She cleared her throat as if she were about to recite a poem. "Well, the house was long and white, with four columns out front." She took a long drag on her cigarette. "Janey and I used to stay in the guest house sometimes for fun. Why, the guest house was twice as big as this." She swept her arm toward the yellowed ceiling. "And the main house had twenty-six rooms."

Then their mother tilted back her head and laughed, which was also part of the story. "We used to rattle around like a couple of dried peas."

Sarah always pictured two dried-up green peas rolling across a hardwood floor.

"Nine giant oak trees lined each side of the drive-way," their mother continued. "Daddy planted them the very first year they bought the estate."

The familiar stories went on for an hour, about how she and Aunt Janey had lived like two princesses. How she had ended up on Sherman Street in an old gray house had never been clear.

Their mother finished with, "Maybe I'll redecorate this house. You girls deserve something better than the attic, for heaven's sake. How would you like a canopy bed?" She directed her question toward Sarah. "And some new curtains. Maybe a lively chintz print."

Sarah allowed herself to think for a minute that she might be getting a canopy bed. "That would be wonderful," she said, though she couldn't imagine how two canopy beds could fit under the slanted ceiling of their room.

Finally, the last waffle had been eaten. Only a little syrup lay on the bottom of Sarah's plate, and her stomach felt heavy. The talking had wound down to a few murmurs and nods when Dad said, "Should we tell them now, Margaret?"

Tell us what? Sarah glanced at her sister to see if she had heard the same words. Were they really going to get new beds? Carlie's tongue had stopped on the tines of her fork, where she was licking away the last drop of syrup.

Their mother sat straight, pushed her plate back and folded her hands on the table. "Okay, you tell them," she said.

"Well," Dad said, "starting next week, your mother's going to have a job."

"A *job*?" Sarah asked. Their mother had always said it took all of her energy to take care of two girls.

"She's going to work in the business," Dad said. "She'll be the receptionist, the bookkeeper and all-around helper." He looked from one girl's face to the other.

"What about Audrey?" Carlie asked, referring to

the woman who already did that kind of work.

"Don't worry about Audrey," Dad said. "Now, this means we'll have to see a lot of cooperation from you girls. Josephine will be here, but during the week you won't have a mother to come home to. And there could be times when we'll count on you to set the table and start dinner. Carlie, you'll have to do the laundry."

Sarah hardly heard anything else after that. She had wished their parents would go dancing every night, but a job would be a thousand times better. She sat in dazed silence, nodding at the details of how life was going to be different from that day forward. Something had happened last night when their parents went dancing, that was clear. What it might have been, exactly, Sarah could only guess.

After they had done the breakfast dishes, the girls raced upstairs. They stood in the middle of their room and grinned at each other, Sarah with her hand over her mouth to stifle the squeals that were ready to bubble forth. First their special night, and now this. Sarah flung herself at Carlie and danced her around the bedroom.

Carlie pulled away. "Well, we shouldn't get our hopes up," she said. "You wait, she's going to spoil it somehow."

Sarah felt the smile slip off her face. "No, she won't. Come on, Carlie, let's be happy."

"I know her," Carlie insisted. "Anyway, I don't

want to do any laundry. There are spiders down there in the basement."

"Then I'll do it," Sarah said. "I'm not afraid of a little spider."

All morning the girls listened to animated chatter coming from downstairs. Their mother was to start work the following Wednesday, after she had shopped for new clothes and gotten her hair done.

Their parents whipped into a fury of housecleaning. Who could tell when she would have a chance to clean again, their mother said. And Josephine, having never gone past her sophomore year in high school, couldn't be counted on to do anything right. Dad brought in his shop vacuum while their mother shook out the ruffled organdy curtains.

Later, he went out and brought back a shopping bag full of little white cartons of Chinese food. Everyone sat around the little kitchen table scooping chow mein, fried rice, sweet and sour pork and cooked vegetables out of the cartons.

"Have some more," their mother said, pushing a box toward Sarah. "There's plenty."

Dad's face beamed throughout the meal. When they were finished, he said, "You girls clean up now and get to your homework. School tomorrow." Then he and their mother went into the living room and turned on the television to watch dancing lessons on *Arthur Murray*.

Life really was going to be different now, Sarah

thought. Maybe this time the good feeling would last. She put the leftover food on a plate and covered it with waxed paper. Then she crumpled the boxes and fit them into a garbage bag.

When they were finished cleaning up, Carlie picked up the paper bag of garbage. The girls' eyes locked before Carlie hugged the bag to her chest and headed toward the back door.

"Can I go with you?" Sarah asked.

"No," Carlie answered.

Sarah felt her mouth sag, and she stood looking at the floor until the screen door bumped. It wasn't that she wanted to go out there, really. She just wanted to know Carlie didn't mind. She was still standing there, motionless, when her mother came into the kitchen.

"What's the matter?"

"It was my turn to take out the garbage," Sarah told her, knowing how silly she sounded.

"Oh," her mother said with a puzzled laugh. "Well, I'm sure there will be plenty more tomorrow."

The lonely feeling from last night washed over Sarah again. She wished she could hear what Carlie and the boy talked about. Probably something mushy—mushy and gushy out by the smelly garbage cans. Why should she care? Sarah turned and started up the stairs, letting her hand glide past the light switch at the bottom without turning it on.

Near the top of the stairs, Sarah stopped at the little window. She peered toward the gas station with its orange lights and the dark smudge of alley. Just as she expected, a boy's silhouette, with its hands stuffed into its pockets, was standing at the corner of the garage.

Carefully, Sarah raised the window and pressed her face to the screen. The garbage cans were hidden from view, but she could hear the soft sounds of talking and an occasional laugh.

She stood for a long while, trying to decipher what they said, until her legs cramped from standing on two different stairs. Finally, giving up, she lowered the window, pulled the shade and dressed for bed in the dark. Then she sat on Carlie's bed and waited.

five

THE GIRLS WALKED together the next morning to the corner where Carlie always caught her bus for the high school downtown. When they passed the gas station, Carlie turned and looked.

"He's probably not there," Sarah said.

"Who?"

As if she didn't know. "Doesn't this Jesse person have to go to school?"

"He sort of had to drop out for a while," Carlie said.

Sarah thought about this for a moment. Why would anyone have to quit school? Was he one of those JDs, a juvenile delinquent? Carlie shouldn't be talking to someone like that.

Sarah shook away thoughts of Jesse. Their mother was getting a job; that meant anything was possible. Who could tell? Maybe if their family had a lot more money, they would move away from this neighborhood and they wouldn't be anywhere near a gas station anymore.

Today the sun was shining and Sarah refused to be gloomy. The sky looked huge and blue, as if it held more air than usual—a good reason for smiling as she skipped along the road.

"What's with you?" Carlie asked. She hoisted her books higher into her arms.

"I decided to be happy today. You have to have a positive attitude."

"Who told you that?" Carlie huffed.

"This magazine." Her sister was not going to ruin her mood. Sarah turned her face upward and squinted into the leaves of a big maple. Watching the golden shapes flutter against the morning sky, she concentrated, trying to catch sight of a leaf at the exact moment it let go of the tree. It was a game she played on her way to school sometimes in the fall.

"Darn." Sarah jerked her head to follow a yellow leaf. "I'm always too late."

Carlie played along. "I see one," she said and pointed.

Sarah watched the single maple leaf drift down and settle softly on the curb. "You didn't really see it fall, did you, Carlie?"

Carlie laughed and shook her head. "Here's the Downtown—see you later." Her bus rattled to the corner, belching its smelly fumes, and Carlie got on.

"Wait for me right here after school," Sarah hollered at the closing doors. "I promise I'll hurry."

She held up two fingers, meaning two more days, but Carlie had already joined the mix of coats and hats and laughing faces on the bus.

Sarah stuffed her hands into her pockets and walked the final block to Jefferson school. At the sight of the rounded brick front that housed the library, her spirits lifted like they always did. Inside the building, she maneuvered around a group of boys in front of the office and headed for the sagging steps that led up to the old part of the school, where the sixth-, seventh- and eighth-grade classrooms were located.

"Sarah!" Kim Nomura, one of the girls in her class, came rushing toward her. She was wearing a red corduroy jumper with wavy blue rickrack sewn to the waistband. Kim always looked so pretty in dresses her mother had made especially for her. Her long, black hair was tied with a matching ribbon.

"Sarah, you've got to come to my house after school. My mom's taking me to the Davenport for a Coke; she said I could bring a friend." Kim smiled so big, it looked like her face would split.

The Davenport was a fancy downtown hotel. Kim was so lucky; Sarah had never actually been inside. But that was the trouble with having friends. They always invited you somewhere sooner or later, usually to their house. And then you had to invite them to yours. "I'd like to, but I've got a lot of chores to do."

"You had chores last week, too," Kim said. "Do you live on a farm or something?"

"Well, no, not exactly," Sarah answered.

The first bell rang and the girls went into their classroom. "Well, call me then," Kim said. "Here, I already wrote my number down for you."

Sarah took the scrap of paper and sat down. "Okay," she said, but she knew she would never call. Every year it was the same. In September she would meet some new girl, someone who didn't know her from before. The girl would want her to go to a movie, go downtown on Saturday or call on the phone. But the thought of someone from school stepping into her life, even for an hour, was too much to think about.

Then by October, the girl would decide that Sarah wasn't very friendly and would find someone else. It was almost the end of October already. Kim would give up soon.

Well, it didn't matter. Carlie was Sarah's one best friend. Lots of people had just one friend. Hers happened to live with her, which made it even better.

Then Sarah thought, *Maybe I can call Kim on Wednesday, after the new job starts. Yes. Why not?* Maybe this year she could have a friend. They could talk after school, before her mother got home from work.

Sarah suddenly brightened and turned toward the chalkboard to settle in for the morning. As she watched Mrs. Lubie write numbers on the board, she felt almost smug, as if she had found the key to some very important lock.

Mrs. Lubie scratched the board with her white chalk. "How are we coming with our equations?" She wrote a problem on the board. "Raise your hand when you have the answer."

Sarah scribbled on a piece of paper. She raised her hand at the same time that Kim's hand went up.

"Okay, Sarah," Mrs. Lubie said.

"X equals three," Sarah said. She glanced at Kim, who smiled at her.

Math was always the first subject of the day, and it was easy. When Sarah worked a problem and got the right answer, it felt clean and neat, like her bedroom when everything was in its place. In math there was never anything poking out the sides or falling off the edge. Sarah would never drop out of school like Jesse.

Just before lunch, Sarah erased the last sentence of a story she'd been working on and wrote different words. This was maybe her best story yet. In it a high school hood knifed a boy who was a juvenile delinquent, leaving his girlfriend sobbing in an alley. Sarah sighed with satisfaction and wrote *The End* at the bottom of her paper.

"Wanna eat lunch together?"

Sarah jumped, startled by Kim's voice. "Oh, okay. I guess so." She put her papers away, and the two walked out of the room together.

Other seventh graders seemed to know Sarah wasn't much fun to sit with at lunch. That was okay; they never talked about anything important anyway. Sometimes they asked her the answers to questions, but that was not the same thing as liking her. Some of the kids stayed away from Kim, too, maybe because she was Japanese.

Did Kim ever talk about anything important? Sarah wasn't sure yet. "I think it's spaghetti today," Sarah said. "I hope they have French bread with it."

"And peas. I hate those green beans, don't you?"

"They're not even green," Sarah said. If you were hungry enough, gray beans might taste okay, she thought.

The girls made their way down the hall to the lunchroom, which was also the gym. The basketball hoops had been folded up toward the ceiling, and tables with benches had been set up all over the shiny hardwood floor. On one side was a special table for two kids who'd had polio and wore braces on their legs.

Sarah and Kim went through the line and picked up trays, then found a bench where there was room for two.

"I looked ahead in our science book," Kim said. "We're going to be doing some real chemistry experiments."

"Really?" Sarah asked. "Are you sure?"

"I even asked Mrs. Lubie. We're going to choose partners. Do you want to be partners?"

"Sure," Sarah said, feeling a surge of excitement. "Chemistry, with test tubes and beakers? I wonder if we'll have to wear lab coats."

Kim brightened. "I don't know, but I'll ask."

Maybe Kim would make a good second-best friend, Sarah decided—after Wednesday.

Carlie was already standing on the corner when Sarah arrived at the bus stop.

"Kim and I are going to be chemistry partners," Sarah announced. "I'm going to call her on Wednesday and maybe go over to her house. Josephine will let me."

Carlie shifted her books to the opposite arm. "I might go to the gas station."

Sarah felt annoyed, but she didn't comment. She glanced toward the blue sky, took a deep breath and started to skip.

From a full block away the sound of their mother's piano drifted through the trees into the air. Sarah stopped in the middle of the sidewalk to listen. "Come on, Carlie," she said. "You have to be happy now."

"Maybe," her sister answered.

The notes danced through the leaves, tumbling down and climbing upward again in dramatic crescendos. Sarah opened the gate and the girls paused outside the living room window.

"Look, she got her hair cut," Sarah said. "And she's wearing a new dress." She stood on her tiptoes to peer in. A cigarette burned in an ashtray next to the metronome.

Their mother sat at the piano bench, her back straight and the skirt of a red dress spread out like an open fan. Her dark hair was now much shorter, exposing a white neck and shoulders. Her elbows moved in and out as her hands reached for the keys. She hesitated for a moment over the last note, then put up a new page of sheet music and began again. The tune sang out crisp and clear.

"She's playing that song," Carlie said. "'Clair de Lune.'"

"This is proof," Sarah said. "She doesn't play that one unless she's in a good mood."

Carlie continued to stare in the window with her mouth slightly open. Sarah looked up at her sister, trying to read her thoughts. She knew she couldn't be happy unless Carlie was, and neither of them could be happy unless their mother was in a good mood. Sarah didn't know what made her father happy; only their mother, she guessed.

Finally, they went into the house and slipped upstairs. The practicing went on for a long time; then the music was replaced by the sounds of pots and dishes and silverware. Soon a truck door opened and closed, and the garage doors banged. Heavy feet came in through the back door.

Sarah and Carlie sat on the floor upstairs with their backs pressed to the chimney and listened at the grate. They heard their father admire the "little" haircut and their mother tell how much she had spent on new dresses. She had bought shoes, too, she said, but they had all been on sale, except the brown pumps. Then they talked about some people their father had hired to polish floors and something about the accounts.

Later, the girls took their usual places in the kitchen while their parents ate alone at the dining room table.

"You'll like the help." Dad said. "They're a good bunch."

"We'll see," their mother answered. "I'm not expecting much."

After dinner of pork roast and applesauce in the kitchen, the girls were clearing their parents' dishes from the dining room when their mother said cheerfully, "Sarah, honey, you can take out the garbage tonight."

A look of panic flickered across Carlie's face, as if she were wondering why her mother would say such a crazy thing. She looked with accusation at Sarah.

"That's okay," Sarah said. "Carlie can do it if she wants to."

"No, it's only right that you should take turns," their mother said. She stood up and dropped her napkin on the table, then moved to the living room with her ashtray. Their father followed.

The girls hurried into the kitchen with the dishes. "What did you tell her?" Carlie whispered.

"*Nothing.*" Sarah looked out the window. It was already dark. "Why don't you just come with me."

"No, I can't. She might get suspicious, then she won't let me go out there anymore."

"Well, I'll hurry," Sarah offered. "Maybe he won't notice."

Carlie nodded and pushed the garbage bag into Sarah's arms. "His name is Jesse. Tell him I'll talk to him tomorrow. Okay?"

"Okay. But maybe he's not even working tonight."

"He's working," Carlie assured her.

Sarah inched out onto the porch. The smells of pork grease and coffee grounds drifted to her nose from the paper bag. She folded down the top and tried to hold the damp bag away from her coat.

Checking the yard, she felt exactly the same way she had felt the night she came looking for Carlie. The sky was black with a few wispy clouds in front of the moon. Again, the leaves of the apple tree rattled in the breeze. The orange lights from the gas station bathed the alley, creating silhouettes of the old lawn chairs and a broken trellis that stood next to the garage.

He would probably think she was Carlie. He

would come rushing over, and then would be disappointed that it was only Sarah. He might even be mad at her. He was a juvenile delinquent, after all.

There was only one thing to do: make a run for the garbage cans and hurry back before anything terrible happened. Sarah felt Carlie's eyes on her all the way down the sidewalk as she hurried along, trying to anticipate the bumpy cracks in the concrete. Approaching the side of the garage, she scanned the gas station lot. Several cars were at the gas pumps.

Quickly, Sarah slipped through the gate in the back fence and reached for the garbage can lid with one hand. She was about to drop in the bag when something moved in the shadows. Sarah wanted to speak, to tell him she wasn't Carlie, but she gasped instead as a dark shape moved across the alley toward her.

six

THE GARBAGE CAN lid clanked when Sarah dropped it back into place. She shrank back against the garage, holding the bag close as if it were a shield.

The shadowy figure seemed to expand in front of her as he drew nearer, his breath curling away from his mouth in the cold night air. His clothes smelled like car oil and gasoline.

"Where've you been?" he asked. His hand reached out, then quickly pulled back. "Wait, you're not Carlie!" But his voice sounded soft, not angry. He laughed. "Oh, you must be the little sister. I scared you, didn't I?"

Sarah gulped. The lights behind his head reduced his face to a flat, featureless disc. "No, you didn't scare me," she countered. "It's just . . . I wasn't sure who you were."

"I'm Jesse. I'm a friend of your sister's." He turned toward the gas station, revealing a straight nose and a gleam of white teeth. He seemed nervous—because he was supposed to be working, Sarah guessed.

"You wanna dump that?" He took the garbage from her and opened the can, then dropped the bag in and pushed the lid down. "There."

Sarah's arms continued to encircle an invisible bag as she stared toward Jesse's face. With the light from the gas station on her, she knew he could see her plainly. "Carlie can't come out tonight. She says she'll talk to you tomorrow."

"Oh, okay," Jesse said, sounding disappointed. "Hey, I know. Wait here a minute? I'll get a piece of paper and write her a note."

Sarah peered around the corner of the garage. Carlie would be at the bedroom window waiting for her. Where was their mother? "I don't know. I have to get right back."

"I'll hurry." Jesse sprinted away and went into the little gas station office. In the full light now, Sarah could see him more clearly. He had heavy, dark eyebrows and a straight mouth. The top half of him looked square and strong, not like her dad, who seemed old and droopy.

In a moment Jesse was back with a piece of tablet paper that he folded several times. "Here, give her this," he said. He put the note in Sarah's hand and squeezed her fingers around it. His hand was warm and rough. "You and Carlie are pretty good friends, huh?"

"We're *best* friends," Sarah answered.

Another car pulled into the gas station. *Ding, ding.* A man came out of the garage area, wiping his hands on a cloth. He looked around. "Jesse!" he barked.

"Gotta go," Jesse said, and he dashed off.

Sarah put the note in her pocket and ran for the house, taking the back steps in one leap. What had he written? she wondered. She held onto her pocket, feeling that she was hiding something terribly important. Had her mother been watching? The television droned in the living room as she flew through the back porch into the dark kitchen and up the stairs.

Carlie stood at the top in her nightgown and bare feet. "Did you see him?" she asked.

"Yes," Sarah answered, out of breath. She'd made it. "He . . . sent a note." She took the paper out of her pocket and started to unfold it, but Carlie grabbed it and went to sit on her bed. Sarah flopped down next to her.

"Don't, Sarah. It's personal." Carlie held the note facedown in her lap until Sarah got up.

"Aren't you even going to tell me what it says?"

Carlie read the words, smiled and refolded the scrap of paper. "Huh?"

"What did he say?"

"Oh, nothing really. What did you think of him? He's nice, isn't he?"

Sarah crossed her arms over her chest. The note couldn't have said *nothing*. "Come on," she pleaded. "I'm the one who brought it to you. You wouldn't even have a note if I hadn't gone out there."

"If you hadn't gone out there, I would have taken out the garbage myself," Carlie pointed out, "and then there wouldn't have been a note in the first place."

Giving up, Sarah jerked her nightgown off the hook and undressed for bed.

Without so much as looking up, Carlie read her note several more times, then slipped it under her pillow. Sarah watched her pat the pillowcase, then carefully lower her head onto the very center. She combed her hair out on each side with her fingers, then folded her hands on top of her chest. She looked dead.

"What are you doing?" Sarah asked.

Carlie's eyelashes fluttered, but otherwise she didn't move.

Puke! This was the dumbest thing Sarah had ever seen! *My darling Carlie. You are so beautiful. I will love you forever and ever.* Sarah filled in the words with her imagination. *Your sister is beautiful, too,* she added.

Sarah's face burned. "Oh, never mind," she said, scrambling to erase such silly thoughts. But she had to read that note. "Hey, Carlie. I have a great idea.

Why don't we have a party?"

Carlie turned her head slightly on the pillow and looked at her.

"Here in our room, I mean, with our food from the cupboard." When Carlie didn't respond, she added, "We've got to eat up all our food. We might not even need the cupboard anymore after Wednesday. And *I Love Lucy*'s on later." Still not getting a reaction, she said, "We could pretend it's a party for Jesse, except he isn't here."

Carlie smiled. Then she sighed. "Okay, I suppose we could have a party."

Sarah twirled around in her nightgown with the torn hem. She could pretend it had bows and ruffles, even if it didn't. As if tuning in to their thoughts, their mother began playing the piano downstairs, lively songs with lots of fast trills and noisy chords.

While Carlie languished on her pillow, Sarah laid out a wool scarf on the floor. In the middle she set two teacups and a smorgasbord of food from their cupboard, including two sticks of Juicy Fruit gum for dessert. Then she propped Otto next to the scarf, against the chimney. "This will be Jesse," she announced. "All we need now is a bottle of Coke."

Carlie looked down at the furry dog with the felt eyebrows and clapped her hand over her mouth, stifling a laugh. Apparently in the mood now, she jumped up, pulled her robe off the hook and put it on. "I'll see if I can get one. They're not paying any attention to us tonight."

"Okay, hurry." Sarah glanced at her sister's pillow and the indentation where her head had been.

Carlie slipped smoothly down the narrow stairs. Sarah watched from the top. The hinges on the door at the bottom hardly squeaked at all as her sister stepped down into the kitchen.

The instant she was out of sight, Sarah lunged toward Carlie's bed and reached under the pillow. She seized the note and ran to hide behind the chimney, where she opened it with anxious fingers.

Jesse had scrawled in blue ink, *Carlie, Hi. I missed you tonight. I hope I can see you tomorrow.* His name was signed with a *J* that covered the whole bottom of the paper, followed by the rest of his name in tiny letters. Was that all? He hadn't said a word about Sarah. She turned the note over, but there was nothing more written. Sarah looked again at his signature, then traced it with her finger. She sniffed the paper. Gasoline.

"I got it," Carlie whispered, "but it's kind of warm. . . . Sarah?"

Sarah's heart nearly leapt out of her mouth as she stuffed the note into the sleeve of her nightgown and stepped out from behind the chimney.

"What were you doing back there? Here." Carlie handed her the lukewarm bottle. "Too bad I couldn't get any ice cubes."

Nearly unable to breathe, Sarah busied herself

pouring the Coke. The note in her sleeve scratched as she held her arm over each cup. The brown soda fizzed over the tops and slid down the sides onto the scarf.

Sarah's mouth felt stuck in an open position. How had Carlie gotten up the stairs so quietly? She watched her sister plop down on the edge of her bed and lean back on both elbows. Sarah stared down at the cups, forcing her eyes away from Carlie's right hand, which was resting just inches from her pillow. Somehow she would have to put the note back.

"Come on," Sarah said. "It's ready."

Carlie got up and joined her. Sarah held her arm tightly against her side.

Downstairs, Dad said, "You about finished playing, sweetie?"

"What's the matter, I thought you'd like this."

"I do. I do. But it's almost eight."

Their mother played another minute, then stopped. Her sheet music rustled as she put it away. The television came on and *Talent Scouts* started.

While chatter continued downstairs over the voice of Arthur Godfrey, the girls sat cross-legged next to the chimney and ate their food. The furnace had come on and the bricks were nice and warm, but Sarah could scarcely enjoy it with the corners of Carlie's note jabbing her every time she moved.

When the girls were finished eating, they stacked the doll dishes. "Maybe you should take the bottle downstairs and get rid of it," Sarah suggested with sudden inspiration.

"I'm not going down there again," Carlie said certainly. "We can hide it in the cupboard."

"Then let's turn out the lights and listen at the grate. Lucy's coming on." Sarah was amazed at the number of quick ideas that were coming to her.

"Okay," Carlie said.

The moment she had flicked the lights out, Sarah slipped the note carefully out of her sleeve. "Here, you can have Otto on your bed tonight." She whisked the dog to Carlie's bed, propped him up against her pillow, then slid the note back into place.

Sarah took a deep breath and joined Carlie on the floor by the chimney. She hated the sneaky way she felt. The note had said nothing, just as Carlie had claimed.

When the program ended, Sarah said, "Let's play Draw-in-the-Dark here where it's warm."

Carlie agreed, and Sarah crawled around, collecting the tablets and pencils hidden under the quilts. She reached into the cupboard for a few crackers, then brought it all to their place by the bricks.

"I know," Sarah said, folding her paper, "since this is Jesse's party, and he didn't get to come, we should draw him."

Carlie laughed. "Be sure to put a gas pump and some wrenches in his hands." She looked toward the little window on the stairwell, as if her eyes could somehow penetrate all the way to the gas station.

"He's probably gone home by now," Sarah filled in.

"No, he hasn't." Carlie folded her hands over her tablet.

"How do you know?"

"Well . . . Jesse sort of lives there. In a little room in the back."

Sarah stared across the grate at Carlie without saying a word. A jumble of pictures formed in her mind—cold, dark pictures. Finally, Sarah whispered, "He *lives* there? How come?"

"You can't tell anyone, okay?" Carlie leaned close and talked in a hushed voice. "His dad threw him out when he was only fifteen. If it hadn't been for Lew . . ."

"Who?"

"Lew, that guy with the mustache who owns the gas station. Jesse was a real hood until Lew said he could come stay at the station."

"Gee, fifteen. That's just what you are, Carlie!"

"Well," Carlie said in a voice abruptly more cheerful, "if that ever happened to us, I'd know what to do. Jesse told me all about it."

Sarah did not want to hear about things like this. She dropped her cracker and leaned away from the bricks. It didn't seem fair that they had a nice warm chimney and food when they weren't even hungry.

77

Did Jesse have a cupboard? she wondered. "Why did his dad kick him out? What did he *do*?"

"Nothing," Carlie said, her lips in that angry, tight line of hers. "They thought he stole a radio and some other stuff, but it wasn't him."

"How do you know?" Sarah asked.

"I just know. Besides, he told me."

Tuesday moved by like a record played too slow. In the evening, their mother took a bubble bath, painted her fingernails bright red, played polkas on the piano and went to bed early. On Wednesday morning, she was already rushing around when Dad called the girls down for breakfast.

"She's up," Carlie said. "I guess she's riding to work with Dad in the truck."

The house felt odd with the radio on, water running and their parents talking in hurried voices. Downstairs, Dad kept smiling while he spooned oatmeal into bowls and poured grape juice.

From the bathroom, their mother called, "Carlie, Josephine will be here by two. She's going to do the housework and start dinner. But don't let her touch my piano."

"Okay," Carlie said.

"And you girls stay right here. Don't be going anywhere."

"Okay," Carlie said again, with a glance toward Sarah. They pulled out chairs and sat down.

"And there's no need for you two to be all over the house, messing things up," she went on. "There's a load of wash downstairs—you can do that, can't you? But be careful with my automatics, and don't be mixing your laundry in with mine."

Sarah shot a look toward Carlie as she reached for the brown sugar. *Don't mix the cooties.*

"Carlie? Did you hear me?"

"Yes, I hear you."

Their mother never addressed instructions to Sarah, which was okay with her.

Finally, their mother came out of the bathroom wearing a pale gray suit over a pink blouse. The heels on her shiny, black shoes were tall and pointed, and the seams in her stockings ran straight up the backs of her legs.

"How come you're all dressed up?" Sarah blurted out. Audrey, the other office lady, had never dressed up, not like this.

"She looks pretty," Carlie corrected her.

"You have to look successful if you're going to be successful," their mother declared. She ground out a cigarette in the sink.

Their father stood by the back door and smiled on.

A few minutes later, their parents left in the truck, Dad in his plaid shirt and work pants. Sarah and Carlie went out onto the back steps and watched the truck pull away, then gathered their school books, closed the back door carefully and walked toward Grand together in the cold autumn air.

New pictures, like little movies, scrolled through Sarah's mind all day. Sweet, irrational pictures of families laughing as they raked leaves together, families playing at the beach, and mothers and daughters shopping together. Things that would never happen just because someone had gotten a job, but by the time the girls met after school, Sarah felt full of joy.

Now that the day had arrived, Carlie seemed to feel the same way. They connected with one look at the sidewalk, then raced the four blocks home. As they rounded the last corner, Sarah could see that the shades were up and the living room window was wide open in spite of the cold in the air.

Before she even opened the gate into the leaf-strewn yard, Sarah could hear the vacuum running and Josephine's voice reaching high over the noise as she sang along with the radio.

seven

THE GIRLS WENT into the house through the back porch. Only the cord to the vacuum cleaner connected the scene to the roar in the living room.

Carlie walked across the floor and looked back at Sarah with a mischievous smile. "Watch this," she said and pulled the plug.

Instantly, all sound stopped, even Josephine's singing. Then they heard the switch click several times. "What in the . . .?"

Sarah and Carlie huddled in the kitchen, holding in their giggles while the cord slithered around the corner.

Josephine hurried through the doorway with a worried look on her face. Seeing the girls, she laughed and picked up the plug. "So, it's you!" she said, shaking it at them. "I thought I'd broken the vacuum on my first day on the job."

Josephine's whole body moved when she laughed. The multicolored stripes in her dress covered a wide shelf of bosom and narrowed to a belt, where it fanned out again over rounded hips. A bright yellow scarf tied back gray-streaked hair.

She opened her arms for a hug and the girls crowded in. It had been months since they'd seen Josephine. The house seemed completely different when she was there—like a movie in color instead of black and white.

"Looks like you two grew up while I wasn't looking," Josephine said, releasing them. "Oh, your mama left a note. She says you gotta do your homework and set the table for dinner. Other than that, what's on your agenda?"

Sarah and Carlie looked at each other. "Agenda?" Sarah repeated.

"I mean, what're you gonna do?" She propped up the vacuum and got a bakery box from the cupboard. "I brought you some doughnut holes."

With another laugh, Josephine opened the box and set it right in front of them on the counter.

"Oh!" was all Sarah could say. There were dozens of shiny brown balls in the box. Should she take just one or a whole handful?

Carlie daintily took one doughnut hole between two fingertips and consumed it without seeming to swallow. Sarah helped herself to one, too—sticky and soft and sweet. They took turns reaching into the box while Josephine poured milk and chattered about her grown-up boys and how they were always taking cars apart in her garage.

"My agenda is I'm going over to the gas station," Carlie said, licking sugar from her fingers. "I met this really nice boy who works there."

"And what about you, pumpkin?" Josephine asked.

"Laundry," Carlie interrupted. "Don't forget you promised to do it."

Sarah frowned. She had said it only to make Carlie happy. "I'll do it fast."

Josephine patted her shoulder. "Good for you. I'm gonna finish my work here and start dinner. Your folks will be home around five-fifteen." She popped one doughnut hole into her mouth, then pushed the vacuum back into the living room, singing again.

Carlie gulped down the last of her milk, put her glass in the sink and dashed upstairs. In just a few minutes she was back down again, dressed in pants and a shirt. "See you later."

Sarah followed her out onto the back porch and watched her sister run across the driveway with her hair swinging across her back. Carlie hadn't even invited her to go along.

She sighed and headed for the basement door, a misshapen wood panel between the kitchen and the dining room. She pushed the bolt back and opened the door, holding her breath against the smell of dampness and dead bugs. The instant she flipped on the light, a brown spider dropped down between the boards of the stairs. Sarah jumped back.

Josephine came up behind her and peered down. "I'm pretty good at laundry," she said. "You go get yourself some fresh air."

When Sarah hesitated, she said, "Go on, it's my job."

"Really? Thanks, Josephine." Feeling vaguely guilty, Sarah changed out of her school clothes and went outside, where she climbed up into the apple tree. From there she could see the gas station and the cars going by on Grand. No Carlie. Well, so what? Sarah had her own agenda, if only she knew what that should be.

Should she invite Kim over to the house? She imagined her new friend looking around upstairs at the slanted ceiling and the chimney, at Sarah's old nightgown hanging on the hook.

No, it would be better to call her just to talk. The number was still in her pocket, and though she'd made phone calls only a few times in her life, she felt sure she could do it. In the house again, her heart pounded as she carefully picked out the numbers, then waited for the ring.

A woman's voice came on the line, and Sarah asked for Kim.

"Just a minute. Kimmie," the voice called, "it's for you."

Sarah felt a smile pull across her face.

"Hello?" Kim's voice sounded odd on the phone,

softer and higher pitched.

"Hi, Kim. This is Sarah Neville."

"Oh, hi! Mom, it's my friend Sarah." Then to Sarah, "Can you come over?"

There it was, the problem. "No, I can't today," Sarah answered. Then thinking quickly, she added, "I have to go to the library."

"I could meet you there," Kim said. "We could talk and check out the same books."

"Oh!" Sarah's heart leapt. "Well . . ." A trip to the library was not really *going* anywhere, so her mother couldn't object. "Okay! I'll get my bike. I can be there in fifteen minutes."

Sarah barely listened to Kim's answer before she flung down the receiver and spun away from the telephone. "I'm meeting Kim at the library," she hollered down the basement stairs to Josephine. "We're going to check out the same books."

"Okay, have fun," Josephine called back.

Sarah pulled her bike out of the garage, stepped on the pedal and pushed off. She whizzed down the street, hardly noticing the houses as she passed, concentrating instead on the library and on her new friend.

She rushed into the stone building to find Kim already waiting just inside the doors. Seeing the girl with her big, open smile, Sarah let go of her worried feeling from earlier. Together they headed for the shelves. "What kind of books do you like?" she asked.

"Not mushy ones," Kim answered. "I like the exciting kind."

"Me, too. Science fiction is my favorite. Do you ever read books about spaceships?"

"No," Kim said. "Are they good?"

"The best," Sarah told her. "Come on, I'll show you."

She found two copies of several books, one titled *Home to Amalthea*. The covers were still crisp and shiny, with a gray-and-white spaceship painted against a dark blue universe.

Sarah held the book to her nose, breathing in the delicious smell of paper while Kim read the front flap of her copy.

"Sounds good," Kim said.

The woman behind the desk marked their library cards and slid them into the pockets inside the back covers.

"Hey, why don't we go over to the park for a while?" Sarah suggested. "We can read out loud there."

Kim agreed and the girls got back on their bikes to ride two blocks. The cold air stung Sarah's knuckles and bit her ears, but the clear blue sky looked brilliant behind the gold of the maple trees that lined the street. They propped their bikes against the fence and settled on a wooden bench.

"We could take turns," Sarah suggested, "every other page."

"Okay, you go first."

Sarah cleared her throat and read, *"David Henley closed the hatch on the spaceship and sat staring at the unfamiliar controls. Something here would get him to the outer planets, if only he could find the right combination."*

Sarah smiled at Kim next to her on the bench. "I told you it was going to be exciting." She read down the first page as if she were sitting in the seat next to David Henley himself, taking off and racing away from Earth, past the moon and past the red planet Mars.

They continued until they were too cold to turn the pages.

"Maybe we can go downtown to the main library sometime," Kim said.

"I'd like that," Sarah said, though she doubted if she ever could. She slipped her library card into her place in the book and said a quick good-bye. Then Kim rode away, and Sarah pedaled off in the opposite direction.

When she got to Sherman, she went past the house to swing by the gas station. There was Jesse, just as she'd hoped, but no Carlie. He looked different somehow now that she knew he lived in a back room. More like them. Sarah turned around at Grand and passed the station again.

On her third trip by, Jesse looked up and smiled. "Hi, sister Sarah," he said. He pulled the nozzle out of a car and hung it back on the pump, then screwed the cap back in. "Slick bike. Where you been?"

"To the library," Sarah said. "I got a science fiction book."

"No kidding?" Jesse took some money from the man in the car and headed into the gas station office. By the time he came back out, another car had pulled up, so Sarah went on home. He knew her name, at least. The thought made her smile.

In the kitchen Josephine was dropping onions and carrots into a pot on the stove. Carlie leaned with both elbows on the table. "I just know he'll get good grades if he goes back to school," she was saying. "Jesse says he can fix anything."

"A man who can do that is worth his weight in gold," Josephine said. *Plop!* In went a handful of potato pieces. "I swear, my son could build a car from scratch."

"Kim and I checked out books about space—" Sarah's eyes focused on the laundry basket sitting on the floor. In it were the girls' clean socks and under-wear, sitting neatly on top of their mother's blouses. Sarah lunged for the basket and started sorting. Had everything been washed *together*?

This was Sarah's fault; she hadn't explained to Josephine. Carlie knelt down to help her, and the two of them managed to fill a paper bag with their own clothes. Sarah felt Josephine's eyes on them, probably wondering what was going on.

They had just finished digging through the basket and sorting when Dad's truck rolled noisily into the driveway. Sarah checked the clock; it was exactly fifteen minutes past five. Carlie took the bag and slipped upstairs.

Their mother's heels clicked up the sidewalk, then made a softer sound as they touched each wooden step. Sarah grabbed a handful of silverware out of the drawer just in time for the gray suit and scent of violets to enter the kitchen.

"You're home," Josephine said, smoothing her dress. "How was your day?"

Their mother slumped. "Exhausting. People are really something, you know it? They call to have their floors done, then they aren't home and don't leave a key." She fumbled in her purse for her cigarettes, found a pack and shook one out. She lighted it with a match from the kitchen windowsill. Then she kicked off her shoes, dropping down to her usual height, and blew smoke out through her nostrils.

"Well, the pot roast is about ready," Josephine told her. She seemed rushed, as if she were picking up on the girls' mood. "I'll be heading home." She gathered her coat and purse from a chair in the living room, said good-bye and left through the front door.

Their mother followed and closed the door firmly after her. Sarah heard the lock slip into place. Then silence. She imagined her mother in the living room, checking the piano for new fingerprints or scratches.

Quickly, she set silverware at the two places in the kitchen where she and Carlie would eat, then went into the dining room with the rest of the utensils.

Her mother was already glaring in her direction. "You must have homework to do upstairs, or something."

"I already did my homework," Sarah lied. Not that she wanted to stay downstairs one minute longer than she had to. It was just that the lie gave her a small feeling of satisfaction, as if something was under her own control.

She turned around when her father stomped his shoes on the back porch and entered the house. There he was, still red and smiling, and Sarah wondered if he had gone around like that all day.

"I'll finish this," her mother said, taking the spoons and forks from her.

Sarah joined Carlie in their room until they were called back down for dinner, both feeling full of doughnut holes. In the dining room, their parents talked about a man named Clive, who was "too stupid to fill out his forms correctly" and had accidentally charged a customer the wrong amount.

"No wonder we never have any money," their mother remarked. "The help is stealing us blind."

"Clive's new," Dad said. "He'll get the hang of it."

"Tt! Don't hold your breath. And the office, Hal. That furniture's sleazy."

"I know," Dad said.

When it was Carlie's turn to take out the garbage, Sarah stood on the steps by the back window and watched, for what she wasn't sure. Tonight there wouldn't be a note, she knew. The notes were only for Carlie. She waited anyway, hoping to catch a glimpse of something exciting, at least of Jesse running back across the alley. The dusty screen bulged with the pressure of her nose pressed hard against it.

"What are you looking at?" her mother asked, appearing at the bottom of the stairs.

Sarah pulled back. "Nothing."

Her mother exhaled with annoyance. "*Nothing*," she mimicked. "I want you to brush your teeth now, so your father and I can have some peace and quiet." She turned to look out the small window in the back door, then opened the door a crack and called, "Carlie! Carlie, hurry it up."

A few seconds later, Sarah saw Carlie come rushing along the sidewalk. The shadow of Jesse moved back across the alley.

When Carlie reached the bottom of the steps, their mother asked, "Who was that?"

"Nobody."

"Don't tell me *nobody*," their mother said, her voice rising. "I'm sick and tired of 'nothing' and 'nobody.' I just saw someone out there."

Sarah held her breath.

As Carlie inched past her to go up the stairs, their mother raised her hand and Carlie jerked away. Her head hit the door, causing the wooden panel to vibrate.

Sarah pulled in her shoulders, waiting for the blow.

"I want to know who was *out there*!" their mother demanded, each word louder than the last.

At first, Carlie said nothing. Then when her mother raised her hand again, she answered, "It was just someone who works at the gas station."

Sarah's stomach knotted as she watched Carlie rub the side of her head.

"He only wanted to know if I'd seen anyone messing with the tires. Someone's been stealing them."

Fast thinking, Sarah thought. Carlie rushed up the stairs and the door closed behind her, leaving the stairwell in darkness. Their mother mumbled and retreated.

"Sometimes I wish she'd get it over with, make me bleed," Carlie said, her hand still on her head.

Sarah felt her insides squirm, and she cast her eyes downward. She knew exactly what Carlie was talking about. She had felt the same way, that most of the hurts their mother inflicted on them were the invisible kind, the kind you couldn't explain to anyone. At least you could see blood. But that was crazy. What she really wanted was just to have a normal family, one like Kim probably had. No way would she ever invite a friend over to this house.

eight

BY THE NEXT morning, Sarah had read to Chapter 5 of *Home to Amalthea,* and she took her copy to school as planned. She rushed up the steps at school, where Kim was already waiting. "Did you read the part where David's tether breaks?"

"Twice," Kim said. "I was so scared when he went floating off into space."

Sarah loved the hard feel of the book binding in her arm; it was as if someone she knew lived inside the pages. And now Kim was reading the very same pages. Sarah and Carlie had never shared books like this.

Kim seemed deep in thought. "Imagine," she said, "what it would be like to just float around in outer space forever. It's so dark out there, and you'd never see your family again."

"I know." Sarah felt a chill at the thought of being separated from Carlie for the rest of time. But the thought was too large to comprehend, and she put it out of her mind.

The bell rang and the girls went to their seats. Sarah smiled across the room at her friend, who smiled back.

After school for the rest of the week, the two met at the library. On Friday, they read the last paragraphs of *Home to Amalthea* aloud at the park.

When they were finished, Kim closed her book and held it close to her. "Wow, that was really good."

"I hate it when books end," Sarah said. "Let's check out another one right away. You pick this time." The next day, Kim chose two copies of *The Ruby Caper*, a mystery about three kids who found stolen jewels.

On Monday, before Sarah left for the library, Carlie went to the gas station as usual. Each day she seemed to move a little faster, until lately she'd been jumping off the steps of the back porch and running across the alley. She never stayed long, but she always raced back with her eyes sparkly and her hair streaming.

"Have you seen his room?" Sarah asked one night after they had gone to bed.

"I saw it today," Carlie said. "It used to be a storeroom, so it's kind of small, but Lew put a truck seat in for him to sleep on, and there are shelves for his things. It's okay really."

"What does he eat?" Sarah wanted to know.

"Lew brings him things," Carlie said. "And I

gave him a bag of apples and the rest of our crackers, the one's that weren't too stale. Besides, it's only
temporary. One of these days he'll have enough
money to rent a real room."

"What does he do, wash up in the men's restroom or something?"

"I don't know, but at least he has a job. I wish I
had a job."

"No, you don't. What would you do?"

"Something."

Sarah forced her mind away from Jesse. "Are
you ready to play a game?"

Carlie shook her head. "I'm too tired."

Sarah was tired, too, but they hadn't played
Draw-in-the-Dark all week. "Just one round?" she
begged.

"No, Sarah, not tonight."

Sarah felt herself sag. She missed playing their
games, and she missed Carlie. She lay with her hands
locked behind her head and watched the leafy pat-
terns on the ceiling. The bedroom window was open
a crack, and the last pictures they had drawn fluttered on the wall above Sarah's head.

On a Wednesday, two full weeks after their mother
had started her job, the girls sat in the kitchen with
Josephine. Rain drummed against the house, filling
the gutters and splashing on the back steps.

"I don't have any agenda tonight," Sarah said. "I

already called Kim, but she can't go to the library."

"Jesse is changing the tires on someone's car," Carlie said. "I think I'll take a bath. Wanna get in?"

Sarah shot her a surprised look, knowing Carlie didn't have permission, but thinking at the same time that life was different now. Their mother wasn't home to say no. Sarah's eyes automatically went to the clock over the stove. Everything was measured now against 5:15, as if life itself fell off the edge and disappeared at that precise time. It was now 4:30.

"Sure, I'll get in with you," Sarah said, jumping up from the table.

"Come on, maybe we can make it a bubble bath."

"We gotta be quick, though," Sarah said. She felt Josephine's eyes on them as they went into the bathroom and turned on the faucet full blast.

Carlie chose the tall lavender bottle from the little shelf above the tub, then pulled out the faceted glass stopper and sniffed. "Mmm. It smells good. But there's not much left in this one." She opened another bottle and checked.

"I wonder what happened to the Pixie bubble bath I got for Christmas," Sarah said. She rummaged in the cabinet under the sink, pushing aside towels and a bag of cotton balls. "Gee, I never even got to use it. Maybe we could use laundry soap."

"That would work," Carlie said, replacing the second bottle. "Hurry, the tub's filling up."

Sarah ran to the basement and picked up the heavy box of Tide from its place next to the automatic washer. A measuring cup lay inside on top of the white granules. Sarah made her way carefully back up the basement stairs, holding the box in her arms like a bag full of groceries.

"Here, it's almost full." She set the box on the floor and filled the scoop with soap, then let it snow into the water gushing from the spigot. As the granules hit the surface, they swirled in circles and sank to the bottom.

"It's not fluffing up much," Sarah complained, leaning over the tub.

"Add some dish soap," Carlie suggested. She stood in front of the mirror, pinning up her hair with bobby pins.

Sarah got the bottle from the kitchen and squeezed it under the faucet.

Carlie swished the water with her hands. In a moment, the surface was covered with white suds that puffed up like whipping cream. "Come on. Let's get in before they're all gone." She dropped her shoes on the floor and pulled her shirt over her head.

When she was completely undressed, she lowered herself into the tub, sloshing the suds up and over the edge. She sank down until only her face and pile of dark hair were visible against the rounded rim. She pulled out one hand, watched the bubbles slide away, and examined her fingernails as if they were manicured instead of just broken off.

Sarah finished undressing and got in, too, grinning at Carlie. She took great handfuls of suds and frosted them up around herself, building a sculpture around her neck and over her shoulders.

Outside, rain hit the little bathroom window and ran down in rivulets. "This is cozy, isn't it?" Sarah said.

"It's really cozy," Carlie agreed. "I wish we could do this every day."

"Me, too," said Sarah. "Hey, Josephine," she called, feeling as free as a four-year-old, "come look at us."

Josephine came through the kitchen and stood in the doorway.

The girls lay among the bubbles and laughed up at her, swishing their arms and tossing soap balls at each other. Sarah didn't care that they were too old to act so silly.

"My goodness," Josephine said. "Don't you two sink down under there. I'd never find you. Maybe I should throw the laundry in." She laughed. "You girls be sure to rinse off good, now."

"What time is it?" Sarah asked.

Josephine went back into the kitchen. "Ten to five," she called. "Better be gettin' out now."

"Okay, in a minute," Carlie said. The television went on in the living room.

Sarah settled back in the tub and swished her

arms through the warm water. She tried to think of when she had been happier than this, but she couldn't remember. A cupboard in the wall was just a vision from a long time ago, before their mother's job.

She looked across at Carlie, who seemed almost to be going to sleep. But her sister wasn't tired, she knew; she was just dreaming about Jesse.

"It must be time to get out," Sarah said.

Carlie opened her eyes lazily.

"We have to pick up everything," Sarah reminded her. "And wipe the floor."

Carlie stood up. "I know." She sounded sad. Globs of soapy bubbles slid down her legs and back into the tub.

Sarah reached behind her to pull the plug, then pulled herself up and ran her hands down her body, shaving off the suds.

A moment later, in their underwear and shirts, Sarah checked the tub, expecting it to be empty. The gurgle of draining water had stopped, but the tub was nearly as heaped with bubbles as it had been before.

Sarah turned the tap back on and watched the water clear a round hole through the suds.

"Try cold water," Carlie suggested.

"It *is* cold," Sarah insisted. "They won't go away." Heart quickening, she began catching water in her hands and throwing it over the bubbles as if she could douse them like a fire.

"Geez! They'll be home any minute," Carlie said. "I'd better get a bucket or something." She ran from the bathroom and came back breathless with the mop bucket from the porch. "We have to hurry. It's almost five-fifteen!"

Sarah stood gaping at the tub as Carlie poured bucket after bucketful of cold water on the bubbles.

"You put in way too much!" Carlie accused her.

"Well, you *told* me to!" Sarah gasped. "We're just making them bigger." She looked frantically around the bathroom for a solution, then hoisted the window, cracking loose old paint. "Hurry—throw them out the window!"

Carlie scooped up a bucketful of suds. A few white blobs hit the windowsill or landed on the floor, but mostly the bubbles stayed in the bucket. Carlie turned the bucket around and looked in. "Oh, no," she moaned.

"What are we going to do?" Sarah could hear the fear in her own voice. The back door was going to open any second, and their mother was going to walk in and see what they had done. Her breath drew short at the thought. With no further ideas, Sarah stepped back into the tub and began stomping as if she could somehow kill the suds, or at least smash them.

Carlie reached past her to turn on the tap and refill the bucket. Water flew. In a panic now, Sarah stomped faster and harder. She scooped the suds toward the drain with the side of her foot and stomped some more. The bathroom shook. The shelf rattled.

Sarah looked up just as their mother's lavender bottle walked to the edge and toppled into the tub. It shattered somewhere beneath the suds.

"Ow!" Sarah jumped and reached for her foot. Luckily, it wasn't bleeding.

Then both girls stood staring into the tub and what was left of the pointed stopper protruding with a shard of glass out of the bubbles.

Josephine came to the doorway. "What's all the fuss in here?"

"Josephine, the bubbles won't go away!" Sarah wailed. "We're in big trouble."

Josephine looked from one girl to the other. "Take it easy. Surely you won't be in trouble for taking a bath!"

"Yes, we will," Carlie put in. "You don't understand."

"But why?" Josephine asked.

"That's just the way it is." The words sounded dumb. Sarah didn't know why. It was just that it had always been that way from the beginning of time. It had something to do with being in her way and the girls being too dirty to share the bathroom.

A moment later, three heads snapped toward the

back door. Through the sound of the rain, Dad's truck could be heard idling in the driveway.

"It's your folks," Josephine said. "You girls run on upstairs. I'll take care of this."

Without taking time to consider, Sarah scooped up her clothes and shoes and dashed for the stairs. Carlie came right behind her, bumping into her, nearly overrunning her. They pushed through the doorway onto the stairs and pulled the door shut behind them. Then they scurried up the narrow flight into the safety of their room.

The screen door on the porch below opened, followed by the door into the kitchen. Staying close to the stairs to listen, the girls put their clothes back on.

Sarah held her breath. Her mouth would not close, but neither could she speak.

"Oh, you're home already?" she heard Josephine say. "I was just fixin' to take those blinds down and wash 'em for you, but I had a little accident."

Silence. Dad's footsteps moved across the kitchen. "What happened?"

The girls looked at each other, and a swallow dropped down Sarah's throat.

"That shelf there," Josephine said. "I guess I bumped it."

Their mother had not said a word, but Sarah knew she was there, taking it all in, judging what had happened.

"Are you hurt?" Dad asked. Josephine must have

shaken her head no. He added, "No harm. A glass jar—it can be replaced."

Then Sarah heard some mumbling and bustling around. It sounded like Josephine was scooping up the glass from the bottom of the tub. Still their mother said nothing. Finally, the three of them moved into the kitchen, then on into the living room.

A few seconds later, the front door opened and Josephine said, "I'm real sorry. I'll see about replacing the bottle."

"I wouldn't hear of it," Dad said. "Do you want a ride home? It's pretty dark and rainy out there."

"No thanks," Josephine said. "I need the fresh air," and she left quickly through the front door. The lock clicked.

Sarah strained at the silence that followed, knowing that it concealed an explosion big enough to make the whole house tremble.

Finally, their mother's voice broke in, low at first. "Well, how do you like that?" she began. "She wasn't cleaning any blinds. There are suds in the tub, and the floor's all wet."

"I know, I know," Dad said, "but it doesn't matter."

Sarah and Carlie moved across the floor, testing each board under the linoleum before they stepped down. They moved in unison as if they were paired in some kind of dance, and knelt down at the grate.

Their eyes met across the space, and Sarah finally closed her mouth.

"That stupid woman," their mother went on, her voice growing sharper. "If you ask me, she was trying my bath crystals. I should have known this wasn't going to work."

Dad mumbled his weak protest. "Now, Margaret. It's not that important."

"Yes, it is!" she yelled. "I can't have this woman in my house!"

Carlie looked up from the grate and whispered, "What's she going to do?"

"I don't know." Sarah felt tears well in her eyes.

"This is exactly what I expected—that witch!" their mother snarled. "I take a job and that woman ruins it for me! Well, you can't make a silk purse out of a sow's ear, that's for sure. I wonder what else she's gotten into. I'll bet she plays my piano, too. Not that she would know how to play it!"

"She hasn't been playing your piano," Dad soothed.

"How would you know?" she shrieked. "You don't care. You don't care about anything!"

Sarah's stomach turned. It was only a matter of time before she called the girls downstairs to testify. But Sarah couldn't fathom telling their mother what they'd done. She couldn't stand the thought of being in the same room and listening to that shrill voice hammering at her. That awful feeling would follow, that they should never have been born. That they were filthy and terrible.

Why had they taken the bath? Sarah wished they could go back now and not do it. In one fateful swoosh, she saw their happy life drain away as if it had been in the bathtub with the bubbles.

"We didn't even thank Josephine," Sarah said. Tears began to roll down her cheeks, and underneath her clothes her skin began to itch.

nine

"WHO DOES THAT woman think she is? I won't have it!" Their mother paced around the house, her voice alternating between grumbling and screeching, until late into the evening. She seemed to forget about dinner again, even though the smell of meat loaf had floated through the vent into the upstairs bedroom.

Every few minutes, Dad said, "Now Margaret, you're getting yourself all riled up," or "It's just a bottle. I'll buy you another one."

Sarah scratched her arm, then her leg. Her skin prickled. She changed positions and willed herself not to move as she listened for her name or Carlie's in the conversation.

Through the little metal squares of the grate she saw the top of their mother's head come into view. Instinctively, Sarah drew back just as the cap of black hair stopped and rotated upward. From where Sarah sat, the face looked pale and distorted, as if she'd been sick in bed for a long time.

"Get to bed up there!" their mother shouted up through the grate.

Sarah sucked in her breath and pushed herself across the slick floor toward her bed. "What?" she answered as if she'd been on the other side of the room all along.

"I know what you're doing up there!"

Carlie sat frozen between the chimney and the grate, her face reflecting a ghostly blue-white from the light downstairs. When her features relaxed, Sarah knew their mother had moved away.

"Do you think she saw us?" Sarah whispered.

"I don't think so." Carlie stood up and moved carefully to her bed. "She would have marched right up here."

The next sounds were muffled. They had moved into the bedroom downstairs.

A gust of wind and rain rattled the windows. At least they were cozy in their room together, Sarah thought. Feeling relieved, she sat cross-legged in the darkness without speaking, but after a few moments, the itch she had felt earlier began to bristle. Carlie must have felt it, too. In the dim light, Sarah saw her sister raise her shirt and examine her middle.

"Ooh, that soap!" Carlie said, scratching her stomach. "We should have rinsed off like Josephine said."

Sarah's hand went to the hollow under her chin where she had piled bubbles like a winter scarf. "We'd better get this off," she said. All at once, every inch of her skin felt afire, as if the soap had just now had time to work. "Is there any water left in the thermos?"

"No, it's empty," Carlie said.

"Then we'll have to go downstairs."

"No, no, we can't do that!" Carlie was silent for a moment, then said, "I know. We can wash off in the rain."

Sarah pictured herself crawling out on the roof naked. "You mean, go outside?"

"Of course not," Carlie laughed. "We can set all the doll dishes outside. They'll fill up with water."

"Carlie, you're so smart." Sarah tiptoed across the room and gathered all the cups and the teapot.

Carlie pushed back the curtains and opened the windows. Instantly, the rain whipped in to sprinkle the front of the girls' clothes.

Carlie stood rubbing her shirt back and forth across her middle.

Sarah lined up the dishes on the roof, carefully arranging them so they didn't touch. Then she closed the windows again.

"I hope it rains cats and dogs," she said, wiggling now from the itch.

They knelt in front of the windows and waited. Rain pelted down, stirring up the leaves that had settled on the roof. With the rain, a new gust of wind blew through the tree. It sent more leaves, tiny twigs and seed pods splattering against the glass. One by one, the wind knocked over every teacup. A second gust sent them rolling off the roof. Carlie opened the window a crack and reached out for the teapot just as the last cup sailed away.

A vivid picture formed in Sarah's mind of the cups seen from down below—doll dishes coming down with the rain. She imagined her mother standing at the front door, trying to figure it out. *Hal, Hal! Come look at this!*

Sarah's chest had been tight with guilt and dread, but now she began to laugh, and when she looked at Carlie, her sister laughed, too. Together the girls slid to the floor and giggled and scratched as quietly as they possibly could.

When they had calmed down, Carlie said, "I have a better idea."

"I'm not crawling out there naked," Sarah said.

"No, but we can put our shirts out there. Then when they get all wet, we can wash off with them."

"Okay," Sarah said, "but we'd better hook them in the window so they don't blow away." Fresh laughter sputtered from her lips as they worked to hook the shirts securely between the two windows. Before long, both were dripping wet.

Sarah and Carlie took off the rest of their clothes and wiped down with the cold, wet shirts. Oh, it felt so good. When the shirts were warm and no longer drippy, they put them outside a second time, and then a third.

Downstairs, the oven door rattled and Dad came to the foot of the stairs. "You girls had any dinner yet?" he asked.

Carlie clutched her clothes to her and shook her head at Sarah.

"No," Sarah answered, "but we're not hungry."

"You sure?"

"We had a snack after school," Sarah said.

"Oh, okay." The door closed.

Sarah heard her father cross over to the stove again, get a plate out of the cupboard and slide the baking dish out of the oven. A delicious picture played in her mind of Dad cutting off a thick slab of meat loaf, then spooning on some of the tomato sauce. She could even see the steam rising off his plate.

"We can't go down there tonight," Carlie repeated.

"I know. Maybe it'll blow over by morning."

"Maybe," Carlie said as if she didn't believe it really would.

"Dad likes going to work with her," Sarah said. "And she likes wearing her new clothes. It'll blow over."

The girls pulled on their nightgowns and got into bed. Sarah's skin felt tight and papery now, but that didn't stop her from thinking about the meat loaf downstairs.

"I wonder if there's anything left in the cupboard," she said, moving Rosemary and Otto out of the way and prying the wall panel loose. She closed her hand on two parcels from the top of the cardboard box.

The first napkin held three graham crackers and the second a few broken potato chips. They should have kept the cupboard full. Sarah remembered Josephine's doughnut holes and how stuffed they'd felt after eating so many. If only she hadn't broken that stupid bottle.

The next morning, Sarah was the first downstairs for their father's oatmeal. The itch had gone away, but her skin still felt tight. She wished she could get into a nice tub full of clear water and wash off properly.

At the sight of her mother in her flowered robe, Sarah's mouth opened. "Aren't you going to work?"

With an annoyed look, her mother picked up a piece of paper folded around a check and thrust it at Sarah. "Here. I want you to ride your bike down to Josephine's before school. Give her what I owe her and tell her we don't need her anymore."

"Oh." Sarah's heart fell. Carlie had been right; nothing had blown over. She stared at the check and closed her eyes for a moment. There was Josephine's face smiling at her, asking about her agenda, saying she'd do the laundry. She felt the sting of tears behind her eyelids and sniffed. This was her fault, hers and Carlie's.

"What now? You aren't crying over that woman, are you?"

"No," Sarah said through her tears.

"I certainly hope not."

Dad, who had been standing at the stove without a word, set two full bowls of oatmeal on the table without looking at either Sarah or her mother. Then he scooped his keys off the windowsill and headed out the back door. "I'm going to warm up the truck," he said flatly.

Sarah watched him move with purpose, as if there weren't a fragment of thought in his head beyond warming up the truck. Her own head swam with guilt for what she'd done to Josephine. Dad pulled the door shut, sending a blast of cold air into the kitchen.

Sarah shivered and turned her attention to the steaming oatmeal. No one was going to stop her from eating this time, she decided, and she plunked down in her chair defiantly. She ate without looking up and without asking for sugar or milk, while her mother moved things around at the sink.

When Carlie joined her, Sarah stared at the check until Carlie got the message and looked down. Then Sarah arched an eyebrow, and she knew her sister understood what she was trying to tell her. *She's firing Josephine—because of us!*

Dad came back into the kitchen. "About ready, Margaret?" he asked their mother in an overly cheerful tone.

In a swish of satiny rosebuds, their mother whirled from the sink. "You can see perfectly well I'm not *ready*!" she accused him. "Why are you in such a hurry anyway?"

Dad's face flushed even redder than usual. "Well, I'm going down to open the shop," he said sharply. "I'll come back to get you later." And he left, yanking the door shut soundly behind him. Sarah's ears followed him as he walked fast to his truck. She clenched her teeth to keep from smiling at Dad's small protest.

"Tt! The floor-polishing magnate," their mother said to the closed door. "Get going now. You're going to be late for school."

You get going. It's your note, Sarah wished she could say. Instead, she got up silently from the table, put her bowl in the sink and went out to the garage for her bike. Before pushing off, she looked down the road toward Josephine's house.

I don't want to do this, she thought. Without Josephine, their house would seem empty and colorless again.

If only she had told her mother she had broken the bottle. She straddled her bike for a moment and stared at the back screen door. *I stomped so hard in*

113

the tub, it made your bottle fall off. It sounded ridiculous. Why would anyone be stomping in a bathtub? *I accidentally slammed the door and the bottle fell off. Carlie and I were taking a bubble bath. . . .*

Sarah should go in there and tell the truth. Then even if something terrible happened, Josephine would be able to come back. But she couldn't. At the very thought of it, her knees gave way and her stomach felt as if she were racing down a hill. She took several deep breaths and pedaled slowly down the road, the note and check stuffed into her jacket pocket. She barely noticed that the front yard was strewn with little plastic teacups.

Her insides squirmed as she rehearsed what she might say to Josephine. She crossed the intersection into Josephine's neighborhood, then rode right on past her house and circled the block several times.

Finally, she rode up the driveway. Josephine lived in a white house with yellow shutters behind a fence of uneven boards. A small, sagging garage occupied the back corner of the property. Sarah leaned her bike against the porch and knocked on the front door. It had been scratched raw by her dog, Ralph, who now started to bark inside.

When the door opened, Josephine stood there in her striped dress, the very one she'd been wearing that first day. Ralph, her big spotted dog, bounced at her feet.

"What's wrong?" Josephine asked. She set Ralph back on his haunches and invited Sarah into the house where she lived, alone. Bookshelves lining two walls were a virtual gift shop of figurines and things made of yarn or carved out of wood. Volumes of Readers' Digest Condensed Books and Zane Grey Westerns with ragged jackets filled in the rest of the space.

Warm and inside now, Sarah felt her chin wobble. "I wanted to tell her the bottle was my fault," she said, fighting tears, "but I was scared. . . . I'm sorry, Josephine."

"Never mind," Josephine said, and she hugged Sarah to her. "I'm glad you didn't tell. I'm not blind. That house is not a happy place." She took the paper Sarah held out.

Josephine read the words and put the check on the bookshelf. "So I won't be coming back." She sighed. "I need the money, all right, but I can live without it. Besides, hey, I need to be free to visit my sons. I'm just worried about you girls." She hugged Sarah again.

"We'll be fine. Thank you for taking the blame. I just wish . . ."

"It's all right. You two stick together now, you hear?"

"Okay," Sarah said, "we will." She bent down and rubbed Ralph's ears. "I guess I'd better go. I'm already late for school. Maybe this will . . ." *blow over*, she started to say, but she raised her arms and dropped them again in resignation. "We had fun, didn't we, Josephine?"

"We sure did, pumpkin."

Sarah could not concentrate all day. Even reading *The Ruby Caper* with Kim didn't cheer her. What she'd done—or hadn't done—was bad, and she knew somehow that she would be punished. The house would catch fire and Carlie would get hurt, or Dad would have a wreck in the truck. Something was going to happen because of the bubble bath.

To Sarah's relief, their mother was not there when she got home. Dad must have picked her up like he said. Carlie went across the alley to see Jesse, but Sarah stayed in their room thinking. She didn't want to go anywhere or talk to Kim. She didn't feel entitled to an agenda after what she'd done, even though Carlie had pointed out that other kids took baths whenever they wanted. Not in this house.

Her misery followed her through dinner and the dishes afterward.

"It was just an added expense," their mother commented about Josephine. "The girls are old enough. . . ."

"The girls can learn to do the housework and cook," Dad said, agreeing with her. "They'd probably love it." After dinner, he left in the truck again. He seemed busier than ever lately. Tonight he was helping another man do the floors in an office building, he said, and he'd be home late.

Sarah sat upstairs with Carlie for a long time, hardly able to talk. Finally, she walked slowly to the head of the stairs and looked down.

"No, Sarah," Carlie warned. "Don't do it. You'll be sorry."

"I have to tell," Sarah said. "No matter what you say, this is my fault. I'll just tell her the truth. Let her yell at me, and then it'll be over." In her mind, she saw her mother's face twisted with anger, but Sarah made her way down the stairs. "Maybe Josephine will be able to come back tomorrow."

"Don't count on it," Carlie said after her.

Sarah crossed the kitchen and crept close to the open bathroom door. Her mother had just taken a bath, and the moist air smelled like flowers. Through the doorway on the opposite side she could see a shaft of soft lamplight. She nudged the bathroom door open farther with a pointed finger and went through to her mother's door. Through the crack she could see a hint of movement and a curl of gray smoke. Her mother was sitting at her dressing table in her robe, brushing her feathers of dark hair.

Sarah straightened herself.

Her mother jerked toward the crack. "Who's sneaking around in there?"

"It's . . . just me."

"What do you want?"

Sarah squeezed her eyes shut and tried to calm her beating heart.

"I said, what do you want?" The door swung wide open and her mother's pinched face scowled at her.

Sarah stood there, exposed. "I need to tell you something," she said, sounding a lot more calm than she felt.

ten

"WELL? SPEAK UP." Her mother set down her hairbrush and waited, her back in a rounded slump. A rosy glow from her pink lamp lay across the surface of her dressing table, where a comb, nail file and hand mirror, all with ivy-decorated handles, were laid out like surgical instruments.

Sarah forced her gaze downward to avoid her mother's hateful eyes. "Josephine didn't break your bottle. It was me. I did it." The words fell from her mouth into the bedroom. Now they were out there, and Sarah felt an awkward sense of relief.

Her mother's eyes widened for an instant, then narrowed. "Don't give me that," she said. "I know exactly what happened."

"But I did do it."

"That's silly," her mother said. "How could you have broken the bottle? You can't even reach the shelf."

Sarah started to explain, then stopped herself.

Her mother stood up and breezed past her, pushing her feet into her slippers as she went. "I'll settle this," she said.

Sarah moved out of her way.

"Carlie, get down here." She strode across the kitchen and grabbed the doorknob at the foot of the stairs. "You hear me?"

Sarah heard the scuffle as Carlie moved away from the head of the stairs where she'd been listening. A moment later she came down and looked at Sarah as if to say, *I told you you'd be sorry.* The girls took up positions together in the kitchen and waited for the words.

"Okay, how'd my bottle get broken? See if you can manage to get your stories straight. I want to know and *I want to know now.*" She gave the last sentence more force, as if she were prying the truth out of Carlie with one of her ugly vanity tools. She glared and Carlie glared back. Without her makeup, their mother's eyes receded into dark tucks like beads sewn into a doll's face.

"I broke it," Carlie said finally, holding her head unnaturally high.

"*You* broke it?" Their mother smirked, then crossed her arms over her robe. "Let's see, all three of you broke my bottle. That's a fine one!"

When the girls just stared at her, she added, "Well, it doesn't matter. I know exactly what happened. Get on upstairs and don't be coming down here again."

Was that all?

"We want Josephine to come back," Sarah said, in one last attempt. "It's not fair. She didn't do anything. I made the bottle fall. I *did*."

"Tt!" Their mother made that familiar sound with her tongue and went back to her bedroom.

She *wants* Josephine to be guilty, Sarah thought. Josephine may as well have played her piano.

After that their parents talked no more about Josephine. The girls came home the next day and the next week to dust and run the vacuum and put dinner into the oven. They sorted and put in the laundry together. Most nights Sarah set both tables alone and studied the cookbook while Carlie visited Jesse.

"He says he's never known anyone like me," Carlie said one day. "He thinks I'm pretty. He says I should never get my hair cut."

Sarah tore chunks of lettuce into a bowl while Carlie sat backward on a kitchen chair and watched her dreamily.

The look made Sarah squirm inside. "You aren't going to marry him, are you?"

Carlie perked up, lifting her chin off the back of the chair. "Probably," she said. "I can't imagine marrying anyone else."

"That will be years and years from now, though," Sarah said.

"Maybe not. He's seventeen and I'm fifteen. Lots of people get married that young." She sat quietly for a minute. "If we were together and we both had jobs, he wouldn't have to live in that little room."

Sarah sliced a cucumber and some celery. She wished Carlie would help, but she didn't ask. She didn't like this kind of talk. If Carlie got married young, that would mean she'd leave home soon. But, of course, she would take Sarah with her, so maybe it would be fun. It would be like all three of them being married. Sarah would still make the salads, except it would be Carlie and Jesse coming home from work instead of her parents.

The vision was easy to hold on to over the next few weeks, with their mother and father so preoccupied with the job. Sarah connected them mostly to the sounds of the truck pulling up, to their comments on something President Ike had said or to a hollered order from the bottom of the stairs. But Sarah stocked the cupboard again, just in case.

One Saturday afternoon, their mother went with Dad to the shop to catch up on the bookkeeping.

Carlie came crashing through the back porch into the kitchen. "Jesse's going to take me out to dinner!" she said, out of breath. "We're going in Lew's truck to get hamburgers and french fries."

"Really? When?" Sarah asked.

"Maybe tonight. Jesse said it's a date. We might even go to a dance sometime."

"What if she says no?"

"She can't," Carlie said, "because I'm not telling."

"You'll get caught," Sarah warned.

"No, I won't. We'll wait till they go out or something."

Good idea, Sarah thought. Listening to Carlie chatter, Sarah was soon caught up in the excitement, too, and she wondered if she would ever have a date. Probably not, she decided. The boys at school didn't even like her.

"What will you wear?" Sarah asked.

"I don't know," Carlie said. "I'll have to figure something out. Come on, help me."

The girls dashed upstairs, and Carlie began trying on dresses and skirts with different belts. She tied bows in her hair and forced her feet into Sarah's shoes.

"I hate these clothes," Carlie said. "Everything's old and awful. I wish I had something pretty."

Sarah wished there were some way she could help, but there wasn't. Her own clothes were already hand-me-downs from her sister. A thought came to Sarah only seconds before Carlie's face brightened with the same idea—their mother's closet must be like a department store of pretty things.

They looked at each other.

"Come on, I'm going to try on a pair of her shoes," Carlie said. "I'll just try them for a second to see how I look."

Sarah held her breath. Would she really dare? Carlie's face registered a feverish look, a new look since she'd met Jesse.

"Okay," Sarah said, feeling a surge of excitement. After the bubble bath, she knew they were playing dangerous games, but the prospect of seeing what was in their mother's closet was too tempting.

"I'll watch for them at the back door," Sarah offered. Maybe she would try on some shoes herself.

The girls hurried downstairs. Sarah went to the back door and looked outside, then checked the clock. Their mother had been gone only an hour so far; she probably wouldn't be home until dinnertime. Together they went through the bathroom to their parents' bedroom. Sarah turned on the little lamp on the dressing table and looked at herself in the picture mirror. Her eyes laughed back at her, big and excited.

The room lay in perfect order, as if it had been preserved in memory of someone who had died. Only a faint scent of violets remained, and the ever-present odor of cigarettes.

Carlie went straight to the closet and stepped inside, pulling the chain that dangled by the light-bulb in the ceiling. Sarah peered in at the facing rows of dresses, suits, blouses, skirts and nightgowns. Dad's slacks and shirts hung on hangers across the end of the closet. Underneath were stacks of shoe boxes with handwritten labels on the ends. On shelves above the clothes were fancy boxes: square flowered ones, round ones, and boxes with little drawers in them. Everything smelled like violets.

Sarah dashed out to check the back door again and returned. Carlie had taken off her blue pants and stood in a pair of tall red heels. In her hand she held the wooden hanger with their mother's crinkly, black dancing dress.

"You aren't going to try on *that*, are you?" Sarah asked in disbelief.

Carlie looked at her with a glow that lighted up her face. Her eyes sparkled, and she smiled so big, all her white teeth showed. Sarah's ears felt pulled toward the back door, but she wanted to see Carlie in that dress.

"Do it," Sarah urged her. "I'll make sure the coast is clear." She ran through the bathroom into the kitchen once more. The driveway looked gray and empty. The only sounds were of the wind blowing through the trees.

Sarah ran back into the bedroom. "All clear."

Carlie zipped the dress up the back. She was slimmer than their mother and an inch taller now. The skirts flared out from her small waist and hovered around her calves. Her ankles, long and thin, tapered down into the red shoes.

Carlie turned in front of the mirror, smiling her huge, white smile. She looked just like a dress-up doll, Sarah thought, the expensive kind in the cellophane-topped boxes. Wouldn't Jesse be surprised if he could see her like this?

"Oh, you look beautiful, Carlie," Sarah said.

"Thanks." Carlie kept turning and smiling and looking at herself from different angles. "Someday I'm going to have a dress like this," she said. "See if I don't."

"You will," Sarah agreed, and she hoped with all her heart that it was true. Carlie was more beautiful than any of those girls in magazines. "You'd better take them off now," Sarah urged her.

"Okay," Carlie said. "You try it on now."

"Oh, I can't."

"Go ahead. We'll be able to hear the truck."

But some instinct sent Sarah back to the porch to check once more. She was not halfway across the kitchen when she looked up and gasped. Her mother's face was in the window in the back door. Dad was not with her. There had been no sound of a truck. Sarah felt herself go weak and her face drain. It was too late to sneak upstairs. This time Josephine couldn't save them. There was not even time to call out to Carlie.

Her mother looked through the window at Sarah and scowled, then opened the door.

Sarah just stared with her mouth open and her ears ringing.

"What are you doing down here?" her mother asked.

"Nothing." She must have caught a bus and come right back home, Sarah thought.

"Where's Carlie?"

"I don't know."

Sarah's ears strained toward the bedroom. She did not hear so much as a rustle of black dress.

"Well, you must have something to do," she said.

"I have a headache."

Sarah moved slowly up the stairs without saying anything more. In a minute, her mother was going to go in her room and find Carlie. Sarah prayed Carlie would get the dress off and back on its hanger and the shoes back in their box. But that was too much. It was impossible. She couldn't do all that without making any noise. And then what? What possible reason could Carlie give for being in there in the first place?

Sarah wished Dad were home or that Josephine were here. Maybe this was the terrible thing Sarah had been expecting after the bubble bath. Maybe somehow this was her fault for not making her mother believe she had broken the bottle.

Sarah heard her mother cross the kitchen, stop, take off her heels and continue on in her stocking feet. She went into the bathroom and opened the cabinet over the sink, probably looking for aspirin. Sarah could hear her own heart pounding inside her chest so hard it seemed to drum against her rib cage. The pounding brought tears to her eyes. Her hands bristled with sweat.

Carlie's scream filled the house. Something hit the wall with a thud.

"You little witch!" her mother screeched, her voice cracking. "My dress . . . my dress . . . !"

Carlie screamed again.

She was beating her. Their mother was beating Carlie!

Without thinking, Sarah whirled and stumbled down the stairs, feeling as if her heart would come crashing through the front of her chest at any moment. What could she do? She didn't know. Something. This time she had to do something before her mother strangled Carlie—or worse. Flinging herself through the kitchen, she saw the table and stove and wallpaper fly past in a blur of colors.

Another bump. "You filthy pig. You sneaky slut!"

Glass shattered.

"Stop it!" Sarah screamed. "Stop it!"

When she reached the bedroom door, Carlie was slumped backward on the bed, the black dress around her ankles. Her arm was up, protecting her face, and her mother's arm was just coming down with the wooden coat hanger.

Sarah flew in front of Carlie. "No-o-o-o!" she screeched, just as the hanger smashed down on her own shoulder.

With the impact, Sarah's breath rushed out of her lungs. She fell across Carlie's legs and slid to the floor, the black, rough skirts of her mother's dress scratchy against her cheek.

Her mother looked down at Sarah, then back at Carlie, her eyes wide and insane. "Look what you made me do!" she shrieked at Carlie. The next words were impossible to understand as she sobbed and screamed at the same time. Then she took a long breath, sucking in air as if she had been under water for a long time. "You witch! Get out of my house!"

Carlie worked her way out of the dress, kicked the shoes aside and ran from the room in her underwear. Sarah followed, clutching her shoulder and catching a glimpse of her own fractured face in a shard of broken mirror over the dressing table. When they reached their bedroom, they sat on Sarah's bed, hugging each other, sobbing, gasping and sobbing some more.

They huddled together, waiting for their father to get home, but he didn't, not until much later when they were asleep in Carlie's twin bed. Sarah slept on the outside in case she had to run for her own bed in the middle of the night. She awoke several times with a jab of pain and fresh tears rolling into her hair.

Sarah didn't care this time that there had been no dinner. She didn't want to go downstairs to look at her again. She knew their mother hadn't cooked anything, even for herself. Neither had she turned on the television. She had stayed in her bedroom, making little scratching noises as she cleaned things up and moved them around.

Sarah heard their father leave again the next morning, Sunday. Had he seen the broken mirror? She crept across the cold floor to her own bed, wincing from the pain in her shoulder. She pulled the neck of her nightgown down and checked. A red-blue bruise ran the length of her collarbone with a trickle of dried blood at her shoulder. She wiggled her arm and stooped carefully to pick up her tablet and pencils, something normal.

The movement woke Carlie, and she sat up in bed. Sarah could see that she had a bruise on her forehead and another on her cheek. "I'm hungry," Carlie said calmly. "What do we have in the cupboard?"

"Lots of things," Sarah said. She crawled up on her bed and stretched toward the cupboard. "Ow!" A cry escaped as she relived the hanger coming down.

Carlie narrowed her eyes and said, "I hate her!"

Sarah swallowed hard. Neither of them had said they *hated* their mother before. "It's Sunday. Dad will be home pretty soon," she said, changing the subject.

"No, he won't," Carlie said. "Besides, he won't do anything. He's scared of her, too."

"No, he's not," Sarah insisted. "It's just that he doesn't notice things."

Carlie looked toward the window and stared for a long time. "I've got to get out of here," she said finally.

Sarah sat on her bed, not saying a word. Tears rolled down her cheeks. She pinched her eyes shut, but she couldn't stop the tears. "We shouldn't have done it. Just go downstairs and say you're sorry. Then it'll be okay," she said. Her voice quivered.

"It's not going to be okay," Carlie cried. "Not ever."

"But you can't really leave. Where would you go?"

"I don't know. Jesse will help me."

Suddenly, Sarah looked at her sister and knew. Carlie had been thinking about this for a long time, she could tell. Her chest ached with the realization. "You aren't going anywhere," she said, trying to convince herself. "It would just make her madder."

"I don't care." Carlie got out of bed and put on her slippers. She strode toward the stairs.

"Where are you going?" Sarah asked, shocked to see her sister walk so heavily across the floor before their mother got up.

Her heart began pounding again, and for a moment she felt as if this were her natural state, as if she were an animal that couldn't let down its guard.

"I have to go to the bathroom," Carlie said, "and I'm going to. I don't care what she does anymore." Carlie charged down the stairs and crossed the kitchen.

Sarah listened, holding her breath, remembering the way she had listened the day before. She listened for Carlie to scream again and hit the wall. But a few minutes later, she heard the toilet flush and Carlie striding across the kitchen again. To Sarah's surprise, there was no sound from the downstairs bedroom.

When Carlie returned, she dressed in her pants and began pushing socks and underwear into her pillowcase.

"You're not going anywhere," Sarah insisted.

"Tell her I have a book overdue or something," Carlie said.

"Come on, Carlie. You can't leave without me."

Carlie stopped packing for a moment and sat cross-legged on the floor. "I don't belong here. She hates me. I'm going to be sixteen years old, Sarah. I never even knew I was pretty until Jesse told me."

"She hates me, too," Sarah offered.

"No, she doesn't," Carlie said. "It's just me. She only hit you by accident. Anyway, I'm not going to let her ruin my whole life. I'm telling you, I'm getting out of here. Jesse says there are places for kids to go. He stayed at a house for a while."

When Sarah heard her mother's familiar morning cough a few minutes later, she felt a wave of relief.

She'll stop her, Sarah thought. Carlie will cool off. This will blow over, and we'll draw pictures about it in the dark.

But Carlie finished packing, tied the corner of her pillowcase into a knot and went boldly down the stairs. Sarah dressed quickly, holding her breath against the pain in her shoulder, and followed in her bare feet. Their mother was standing in the kitchen, looking pale and pinched, as if she were too tired even to speak.

Sarah looked at her, then rushed out the back door. Carlie had wheeled her bike out of the garage and sat at the curb with her pillowcase draped over the handlebars. Seeing her, Sarah felt as though her mind would splinter. Carlie really was leaving!

Her thoughts zigzagged somewhere behind her eyes without connecting to tell her what to do. Her heart slammed in her chest once more and rang in her ears.

Her mother came to the back door. "What's going on?" she asked in a slow, lazy voice.

Carlie looked up and locked eyes with Sarah. *Don't tell*, she seemed to be saying. But Sarah knew she had to tell. She couldn't live without Carlie. Carlie had always been there, every single day since Sarah had been born. Pictures flashed through her mind, of their bedroom and the cupboard and their doll dishes and the two of them walking home from school.

"You have to stop her," Sarah pleaded, turning to her mother. "Carlie's running away."

Her mother looked toward the street at Carlie. "Tt! Let her go. The little fool, how far does she think she'll get?"

"No. You can't let her go!"

Carlie had hesitated, but now she set her mouth in a straight line and pushed away from the curb.

Sarah could think of nothing else to do but run after her. Her bare feet flew down the walk, out the gate and across the gravel. She hardly felt the sharp rocks beneath her feet or the strain on her shoulder. She would catch her sister and pull her bike back. She would wrestle Carlie to the ground and hold on to her.

"Carlie!" she screamed. But Carlie kept going. Her blue jacket billowed out behind her. "Carlie!"

Then finally, Sarah stopped, her chest burning. "Carlie!" she cried. "Wait! What about *me*?"

eleven

SARAH RAN BACK to the house. Her chest heaved and the bottoms of her feet stung. Her mother had gone inside and was slumped on the couch, with smoke curling away from her right hand.

"She's gone!" Sarah cried at the doorway to the living room. "We have to do something. We have to call the police or tell Dad—or something!"

Her mother stood up just enough to reach out and change television channels.

"Don't you even care?" Sarah cried, choking on her own words.

Finally, her mother turned slightly, and without really looking at Sarah said, "That silly thing—she'll be back soon enough."

Sarah tried to think what to do. Her mind felt fuzzy. Her panic inside did not match the way her mother was sitting so calmly in front of the TV. "Well, I'm going to put on my shoes and go after her."

"You're not going anywhere," her mother snapped. "Get yourself some breakfast. She's doing this to me, to see if she can get me riled up."

Sarah was plenty hungry, but if Carlie wasn't there to eat breakfast, she didn't want any either. Besides, her mother hadn't cared yesterday whether they ate or not, so why should she care today? "I'm not having breakfast," she said boldly.

"Then you can get busy on your homework or clean your room."

Sarah felt a twist in her stomach, and she considered going after Carlie anyway. But she hesitated, feeling as if her mother held her by a rope so tightly that she couldn't move.

Finally, she went with defiance into the bathroom, examined her bloody shoulder in the mirror and gently washed it with a cloth. It wasn't broken, she guessed, but it looked like chicken parts before they were cooked—yellowish with spots of red and blue. When she was finished, she squeezed the cloth into a ball and left it on the side of the sink without rinsing it out. Let her find it. Let Dad find it. Sarah didn't care.

She went back upstairs. Maybe there she would be able to think more clearly. Maybe Carlie would just go around the block a few times, then come back home.

Sarah knelt in front of the double windows in their room to watch the road out front. Most of the leaves had fallen off the maple tree, leaving bare limbs and a nearly clear view.

From their cupboard, she got a waxed bag of saltines, broke off pieces and tossed them into her mouth. If Carlie didn't come back soon, all this great food would be hers. She laughed, but the thought of being alone made her feel sick inside.

She watched the street until the crackers had all been eaten. Only one car went by, and a brown-and-white dog. Sarah moved to the back window. She saw Lew, the gas station owner, dump something into a big barrel. His breath formed a cloud in the cold air, reminding her that it was too cold for Carlie to be out there very long.

Again at the front window, she watched and waited. This was the dumbest thing Carlie had ever done. Sarah crossed her arms angrily over her chest. "Just quit it, Carlie," she said out loud. "You're going to be in terrible trouble." She imagined her on her bike somewhere with her mouth tight, not even thinking about the cold.

In midafternoon, the telephone rang. Sarah rushed to the grate to listen. Her mother answered and a moment later hollered, "Sarah, telephone."

Sarah jumped up and hurried downstairs. Maybe it was Carlie. But no, her mother would have known that, unless she had disguised her voice somehow. Sarah took the receiver her mother held out, avoiding her eyes.

"Make it quick."

"Hello." The voice on the other end belonged to Kim. She wanted to know if Sarah had done her math yet and if she knew there was another David Henley book at the library.

Her mother watched her from the doorway to the kitchen, sucking on her cigarette and blowing her smoke into the room.

"I can't talk right now," Sarah said. "We're expecting a very important call." When she hung up, she knew Kim must be puzzled by her cool tone.

"What have I told you about phone calls?"

Sarah fit herself through the doorway past her mother. "I can't help it if someone calls *me*," she snapped.

"Watch your mouth, young lady. I asked you a question."

"You told me not to tie up the telephone." Sarah hesitated in the kitchen, not yet dismissed.

"Then tell your friends not to call."

"I don't have any friends." Sarah felt her lip quiver. How was she ever going to have any friends with a mother like this?

Her mother sighed. "Help me fix some lunch," she said. "You haven't eaten all day."

Oh, yes I have. Sarah lifted her head and moved to the sink. *We made a new cupboard, and it's better than the first one.*

In jerky motions, Sarah stirred water into a can

138

of tomato soup while her mother got out crackers and sliced some cheese. Sarah set a place for herself at the kitchen table.

Her mother ladled soup into two bowls. "We'll eat in the dining room."

"I like it here." Sarah looked up at her mother's face, daring her to do something that would push her out of the house, too.

"Suit yourself," her mother said with a shrug. She pulled out a kitchen chair and sat down at the one place, arranging her robe over her knees.

Sarah got out another spoon and ate without speaking, aware every moment that her shoulder still ached. She felt angry, angry with everyone. She was angry with Carlie for being gone so long. She was angry with her father for never noticing anything. And she was angry with her mother for . . . all of it.

She kept her eyes downcast as her mother dipped her spoon into her soup, touched it to the edge of the bowl with a little clink and tipped it into her mouth. *Clink. Slurp. Clink. Slurp.* It was the only sound in the room, except for the chewing inside Sarah's own head.

"The holidays are coming up fast," her mother said, as if she were trying to be friendly. "With this job I suppose I'll have to shop on the weekends."

Sarah took a bite of cheese. She was not going to talk to her mother. She's going to ask questions about Carlie next, she thought. She probably wonders how many of her dresses Carlie tried on. *We tried on every single thing in your closet: the shoes, the nightgowns—everything!*

Her mother finished eating and put her dishes in the sink. When she turned toward Sarah, she looked embarrassed, shaky. "You know," she said, "you're part of this family whether you like it or not. What goes on here is private. I expect—"

"I know," Sarah said sharply. *Don't tell.* Another rule, though this one had always been there, unspoken.

Her mother looked away. "You'd better go get your homework done," she said with a sigh, and finally, Sarah climbed the stairs to her room.

She waited upstairs the rest of the day for something to happen. Anything to shake up the silence and stillness in the room. If only her sister had just hidden under the bed or gone to the library. Who was Sarah supposed to talk to now?

Just as darkness enveloped the tree outside the window, the telephone rang again. It wouldn't be Carlie, she knew, but maybe it was Dad. Her mother would tell him what had happened, and he'd come right home.

Again, Sarah listened at the vent. It was her father, all right. Her mother complained about him working on Sunday and asked how long he would be, but that was all.

With a renewed surge of anger, Sarah opened her bedroom windows and leaned out into the cold. She looked up and down the street, then closed the windows again quickly. Where could Carlie have gone? She must be inside somewhere. But where?

As Sarah thought about Carlie's words and the determined way she had pushed off from the curb, an idea came to her. Maybe Carlie had gone to the gas station after all. No one would see her if she was hiding in Jesse's little room.

Energized now, Sarah wadded up the cracker bag and checked around her for other trash. Her mother had said she should clean up their room. That meant there would be garbage that she would have to take out.

Sarah pulled several pictures off the walls, picked up a holey sock and added a couple of old catalogs. She filled a brown paper bag, then took it downstairs, feeling suddenly better.

Her mother was watching television again. "What now?"

"I cleaned my room," Sarah said from the doorway. "I'm going to take out the garbage."

Her mother made a sound that seemed to give permission, and Sarah slipped into her jacket, pushing her arm carefully into its sleeve. Against the blackness of the night were a slit of moon and a spattering of stars. The frozen grass crunched beneath her feet. In her mind she saw Carlie looking at a magazine and eating a candy bar, cozy as could be.

She reached the garbage cans and clanked the lid several times. When no one noticed her, she dropped her bag into the can, replaced the lid and walked boldly across the alley. "Hi, is Jesse working?" A boy she had not seen before was hammering at the wheel of a truck.

"Jesse? I'll have to get him." He loped away and came back a moment later. Jesse was right behind him.

"Hey, sister Sarah. What's up?"

Sarah motioned for him to follow her to the tire bins. "Tell Carlie she's got to come home," she said, keeping her voice low and calm. "She's going to be in big trouble if she stays out all night."

"What do you mean, out all night? Where'd she go?"

"Come on," Sarah said. "She has to be in your room."

"Look, I was just in there. I'm telling you, I haven't seen her."

He was not lying, Sarah could tell. She held her collar under her chin. The cold seeped right through her coat, chilling her bones. "She said she was running away this morning, and she took her bike . . ."

"Oh, geez," Jesse said. His hand clutched the back of his neck. "What happened over there? Your mother?"

142

"Yeah," Sarah said without filling in the rest. "What should we do?" She had done everything wrong, it seemed, and now it was getting so late. "I should have gotten on my bike and followed, but . . ."

"Isn't anyone looking for her? You know, you're going to have to tell someone about your mother sooner or later."

"My dad's not even here," Sarah explained, leaving her mother out of it. "Do you think she went to that home? You know, the one where you stayed?"

"I hope not," Jesse said. "It's just for boys, mostly greasers who've been in trouble. And they don't let you sleep the night. It's just a place to get something to eat and talk to a minister."

"Oh," Sarah said. "Carlie thought . . . She didn't know that. I'm really scared, Jesse. She's been gone all day. What if she got lost?" Her eyes stung, and she pinched them shut.

"Look," Jesse said. "Lew will be back in the morning. Maybe I can use his truck then. There are a couple of places I could look. And I could ask around."

"But we have to do something *tonight*," Sarah begged. "It's freezing out here. Doesn't anybody care?"

"Look, you don't understand. A person isn't officially missing till they've been gone awhile." At first, his voice sounded harsh. Then he softened. "Tell you what. If I find out anything, I'll pitch some gravel against your bedroom window, okay?"

"Promise?"

"I promise. I'm hoping she'll show up on her own, though. She doesn't know what she's getting herself into."

"You don't know how stubborn she is," Sarah said. "Wait. . . I have another idea. Maybe she went to Josephine's. Can we call?"

"Sure, come on."

In the tiny office, Sarah looked up the number, then pushed the phone book toward Jesse. "You call her," Sarah said. "She'll listen to you."

Jesse dialed and waited while the phone rang and rang. Then he hung up and dialed again. "No one there," he said, setting the receiver in its cradle.

Sarah was out of ideas.

"She'll come back," Jesse said as if he knew that was true.

Sarah nodded. "Yeah." With a wave, she ran back to the house, grateful for the warmth inside, and at the same time feeling guilty for the warmth. If Carlie was cold, Sarah felt like she should be cold, too. She draped her jacket over the hook and went back upstairs to sit in the dark by the window.

Later, her mother called her down for dinner. Why was she cooking again? It was almost as if she was glad Carlie wasn't there, as if one kid was okay, but two were just too much. Well, Sarah wasn't

144

going to be her only kid, all happy and lovey. She would eat, but she wouldn't speak.

She wondered about the missing-person rule. Maybe the police gave people a head start so they could get away.

Stepping into the kitchen, Sarah locked eyes with her mother, until her mother turned away and sighed. *She can't figure out what I'm thinking,* Sarah thought. *My thoughts belong to me and no one else.*

This time, without a word, her mother took her plate and her cigarettes into the living room while Sarah took her usual place in the kitchen. She looked down at the plate of chicken à la king without appetite. Her stomach felt too fluttery to eat, and she was beginning to feel feverish. She looked around the kitchen, trying not to notice the empty chair beside her, and at the same time listening for Jesse's pebbles against the window upstairs. She could not think past tonight.

Upstairs again, Sarah stared at her math book without doing a single problem. She would have to go to school tomorrow without her assignment. Mrs. Lubie would wonder what had happened. *My sister ran away and I couldn't think.*

Oh, really? Now, why would she do a thing like that? Sarah could never tell Mrs. Lubie about her family. Her teacher wouldn't care, and besides, those things were too private.

Finally, about nine o'clock, Dad's truck pulled

into the driveway and the garage doors opened. Sarah hurried to the grate and flopped down on her stomach, wincing when she jarred her shoulder.

Her father came in talking about stripping the floors in a bank. "There are four more businesses in town that might need us," he said cheerfully.

"I told you so," her mother said. "Commercial is where the money is." They talked while she dished up his dinner, and then they went into the dining room.

Sarah's ears were primed for her mother's words. She would probably slip them in while her father was eating. *By the way, Carlie ran off. I suppose we should go find her.*

But her mother said not a word about Carlie. Sarah listened for a long time, until she understood that her mother wasn't planning to tell. How could she not be worried about Carlie out there in the cold? Everything Sarah had ever suspected came crowding into her mind. She doesn't love us, she thought clearly. *She really doesn't love us.*

With a gasp, Sarah was suddenly aware of her weight on the metal grate, as if at any moment she could fall straight through. It wasn't that she'd never considered the idea of not being loved before, it was just that she had always come to the same conclusion: mothers *have* to love their kids, so their mother must love them even if she didn't know it. Sarah had always assumed that their mother's feelings were just buried too far down to be found.

But now she understood differently. A mother who didn't want to get her own daughter back must not love her after all. And if their mother didn't love Carlie, her very first child, then she couldn't love Sarah either. It was no different than a math problem: when you subtract everything, there's nothing left. A big, fat zero.

Okay . . . well, it didn't matter. It didn't matter because Sarah loved Carlie more than anything, and she wasn't going to let her sister freeze to death out there, stubborn or not. If her mother wouldn't tell Dad, Sarah would have to somehow.

With angry determination, she crept down the stairs and stood in the kitchen. Except for the glow from the TV in the living room, the room lay in tones of charcoal gray.

She stopped for a moment to grope for words. She couldn't tell her father about the dress and the hanger or about her own shoulder. He might get angry. Their mother's private bedroom was his, too, after all.

Sarah crept across the kitchen floor and stood at the doorway, trying to calm her beating heart. The girls had been told plenty of times not to bother their father the minute he got home, and they'd always assumed the rule was hers. But what if he was the one who didn't want to be bothered?

Then Sarah thought about Carlie out there alone somewhere in the dark and the cold. By now someone could have done something to her. And Jesse himself had said the downtown house wasn't so good. In the end, Carlie would be glad Sarah had told and Dad would be glad she had bothered him.

Sarah stepped out into the dining room and stared at the back of her father's gray hair. As she rocked from one foot to the other, the old hardwood floor creaked. Dad looked over his shoulder.

Her mother turned and looked at her, too. Her eyes, narrowed into dark, angry slits, seemed to shoot a warning toward Sarah. "What do you want?" she asked.

"I just came to say good night." Sarah looked right at her father's face, willing him to understand her message.

"Good night." He turned back toward the television. "You and Carlie sleep tight," he said mechanically. "Tomorrow starts another week."

Sarah took a deep breath. "Carlie's not here," she said, barely able to get the words past the rock in her throat.

Her mother's eyes widened.

"Kind of late to be out, isn't it?" Dad said.

Her mother suddenly stood and picked up her father's plate and silverware. "That silly thing got mad and went to spend the night with one of her little friends."

"Oh? What friend?" Now Dad turned full around.

"How should I know?" her mother said. "She's going to be in plenty of hot water when she gets home, that's for sure."

"Well, let's hope she gives us a call," Dad said. "Sarah, do you know where she's staying?"

Sarah gulped. What could she say that would be true, but not too true? "She's not staying anywhere," she said.

Her mother brushed past her on the way to the kitchen. "Of course she's staying *somewhere*," she said. "What are you trying to do? Get your father all upset for nothing?"

Dad did look worried, though. At first he sat in silence, watching Sarah as if he were waiting for her to explain. Then he leaned forward in his chair and strained toward the kitchen where her mother was rinsing the dishes noisily. His ruddy face was set in a scowl, as if he were trying to figure it all out. But Sarah couldn't tell him any more. She had already said as much as she dared without tattling on her mother.

twelve

"WAS SHE MEETING someone?" Dad sat in his chair, rubbing the rounded arms. "Did she have permission to stay out late?"

"She wasn't meeting anyone." *She ran away. Carlie ran away!*

Her father hoisted himself out of his chair and went to the telephone. "I don't like the sound of this." He flopped open the phone book, then dialed some numbers.

Sarah's heart leapt. If her father thought this was serious, too, then she knew he'd do something.

"Yes, hello," Dad said. "I have a fifteen-year-old daughter who hasn't shown up tonight." He punctuated the sentence with a note of nervous laughter. "Okay, thank you." He stood with one hand pushed into his pants pocket as he waited.

Sarah held her breath so she wouldn't miss anything. She could tell he was talking to the police.

Her mother came to stand in the doorway, her

mouth working angrily as if she were trying to form words she didn't know.

Dad repeated the sentence and added that Carlie could be staying with a friend. "I see. But . . . okay, I see. Yes. Her name is Carlisle Anne Neville. . . . I'm not sure." He covered the mouthpiece. "How tall is Carlie?" he asked their mother.

When she hesitated, Sarah answered, "Five-five and a half."

"Five-five and a half," Dad repeated. "She has green eyes and long, dark brown hair. She's a real pretty girl."

Her mother rolled her eyes toward the ceiling. She shifted her weight and yanked at the strap of her robe as if she were boiling inside. At Carlie. At Sarah herself. What would happen to them if Carlie suddenly walked in the back door?

In her mind, Sarah saw her sister with her eyes closed and her hair splayed out on a pillow. Last time she had seen her like that, she'd been hiding a note and dreaming about Jesse. She had looked dead, Sarah remembered. It had been kind of funny then, but now that image jumped forward with new meaning.

Dad talked a minute more, then hung up the phone. "Well . . . the police officer said there isn't much they can do tonight. He said teenagers tend to hole up with friends and then show up the next day." He looked pleased as he added, "Especially if

151

they come from a good solid family that's never had any trouble."

"See? What'd I tell you?" her mother said, lighting another cigarette.

But Sarah knew Carlie didn't have any friends, not really. No one except her and Jesse. "So, they aren't going to do anything?" Sarah asked.

Dad looked concerned again. "I guess not, although the officer did say they'd keep an eye out for her." He sat back down in his chair. "I can't figure out why she'd do something like this. Maybe she'll call," he concluded. "She will. I'm sure she'll call. Then we can all relax."

"It's selfishness," her mother said. "That's all it is—thinking of herself and no one else. It'll do her good to spend a night out there. Then maybe . . ."

"Margaret, please."

With Dad's words, her mother stopped talking abruptly. For an instant, silence balanced itself in the room like a brittle china plate. Sarah glanced from one parent to the other.

Her mother tightened her bathrobe strap again. "Sarah, get on to bed."

Sarah didn't want to go to bed now. She looked hopefully toward her father.

"'Night," he said. "I'll let you know if we hear anything."

Sarah hesitated. If only she could tell, just open her mouth and tell Dad everything about Carlie and why she had left. But she couldn't; things just weren't done that way in this family. She climbed the stairs alone, feeling a sad weight in her chest.

Sarah moved through their room, past the white chimney where she and Carlie always sat together. It was the same room, with clothes and books strewn around, except it seemed unnaturally still without Carlie. Sarah sat down on the edge of her bed.

So far she had avoided looking at Carlie's side of the room. But now, she glanced across the short space. Her sister's bed was still unmade, the covers thrown back as she had left them this morning.

What if Carlie never came back? What would Sarah do in this room all by herself? The part about being a solid family . . . Sarah wasn't sure what that meant, but she didn't think their family was solid. How could Dad think it was? Yet the television was on again now, as if everything were just fine.

Sarah turned out the light and got into bed, sitting up against her green headboard. She didn't care that *Television Playhouse* had just started. Lying on the floor by the grate to listen would be no fun without Carlie. But she had never slept alone in this room before, either. There had never been summer camp or a visit anywhere. They had always been together, to talk whenever they wanted.

Now the words came back to her like echoes that had been sealed into the room. *Come on, Carlie, please can't we play just one round of Draw-in-the-*

Dark? What did you get to eat, Carlie? Hurry, the cupboard is open. Oh, look, Carlie, the leaves are beginning to fall off the trees. Let's ride our bikes through the park to the library.

Sarah felt the corners of her mouth drag downward. "I am not going to cry," she said, already sniffing. But she did cry. Tears spilled down her cheeks until her nose felt huge and stuffed.

Sarah sat in bed sniffing and blowing her nose, a sense of anger growing inside her. "Maybe you're just hiding out in the garage," she said aloud to the mound of covers on Carlie's bed. "Or maybe you're waiting until they go to sleep so you can sneak in. Of course, you don't have the key. If you come back to the house during the night, you'll be locked out. Well, too bad. You should have thought of that."

This last picture stayed with Sarah for a long time, of Carlie circling the house in the dark, trying to figure out a way to get back in. In her mind, her sister stopped beneath the little window by the stairwell and looked up. "Sarah, Sarah," she would call in a loud whisper. "Come let me in." But Sarah might just be too sleepy to get up.

It felt better to be angry than sad, Sarah decided. Still, she couldn't stay mad at her sister when she remembered Carlie slumped on her mother's bed with that hanger coming down.

"But I'm the one who got hurt," Sarah said out loud, touching her shoulder. "You could have thanked me for getting in the way for you."

She was angry *and* sad, that's what it was. Angry and sad and scared. And she wanted to *do* something, not just sit here and wonder.

Sarah got up and went to the back window, then to the front window. It was too dark to see anything. Finally, she went to Carlie's bed with an idea. There was one thing she could do. She pulled the quilt off her sister's bed, wadded it into an armload and went to the stairwell. Carefully, she raised the window and unlatched the screen. Then she stuffed the quilt out into the cold night. Below, the ivy rustled and Sarah leaned out to see the heap of patterned fabric lying there ready to be picked up by someone who needed it.

Sarah went back to bed, but as the night deepened, she pulled her blankets more tightly around her. Dark, ugly thoughts had crowded into her mind. She saw her sister searching in garbage cans for food and murderers waiting in every shadow to grab her.

Sarah stared wide awake toward the ceiling until her eyes felt so dry and cold, she had to close them. She couldn't think anymore. She couldn't cry. And finally, she was too tired to worry anymore. She went to sleep feeling as if she were fading away into gray nothingness.

Sarah awoke hours later to a sound in the darkness. She jerked up onto her elbows to listen. "Carlie?"

155

But no one was there. Was it Jesse, then? Had he thrown some gravel?

Scritch!

There it was again.

Sarah listened without breathing. The sound was coming from the wall beside her.

Scritch, scritch! Scritch, scritch!

With a start, Sarah drew away, clapping her hand to her chest. The rats! They must have come for the food in the cupboard, just like their mother had warned. She flung back her covers and plunged across the space to her sister's cold bed.

"Girls . . . um, Sarah, time for school." Sarah's eyes opened on the wrong side of the room with her arms clutching Carlie's pillow. Her father was at the bottom of the stairs, calling them like he did every morning, except for an instant he must have forgotten Carlie wasn't there.

Sarah dashed for her own bed. "Okay, I'm awake," she called back.

When the door closed, she went to the back window, opened it and looked down. The quilt was still lying there in a heap, though it looked damp and flatter now. Well, it was still a good idea, Sarah thought. And today was another day. Something new would happen. She got dressed quickly, feeling much better than last night.

"How about a ride to school?" her father asked

156

when Sarah went downstairs for breakfast.

"Okay."

"I'll drop you off and then check in at the high school. Someone there will know who your sister's friends are. Maybe she did spend the night with someone and will show up at school."

"I hope so," Sarah said, although she knew better. While her father was brushing his teeth, she dashed outside to get the quilt, then stashed it behind the trunk in the garage. She pulled one corner out, just in case, so Carlie could still find it.

When they got into the truck, Dad patted Sarah's knee. "Don't worry about your sister," he said. "I just know she's fine."

No, you don't know anything about Carlie, Sarah thought.

After that, he drove along in silence, looking flushed and worried. It was official now—Carlie had been out somewhere all night long. What must she be thinking this very moment? Was she awake yet, or had she even found a place to sleep?

Sarah looked at the side of her father's face. Again, she wanted to tell him everything about why Carlie had left, but what was the use? He wouldn't get it. What she needed was one perfect sentence that would explain everything.

His big hand rested on top of the steering wheel, turning with it as he took the corner. Gray hairs lay along the cuff of his jacket—grown-up man hairs, strong man hairs. Except her father was quiet and red faced, not strong like she had once believed all dads were. He pulled on the brake and waited for her to get out. "Study hard," he said. "Don't worry." Then he was gone.

Study hard? How could she even think about school?

Because of the ride, she had arrived at Jefferson earlier than usual, and she waited in the hallway for Mrs. Lubie to unlock their room. Kim came in a few minutes later with a group of other kids.

"Hey, what's going on?" Kim whispered, dropping a book onto the desk next to Sarah. "Did you get your important phone call?"

Kim's face was like a bright, smiley sun. Sarah knew she shouldn't tell things about her family, but she wanted to talk to someone, and Kim looked so friendly this morning.

"Promise you won't tell?"

"I promise," Kim said.

"Well . . . my sister ran away yesterday."

Kim gasped. "Oh, my gosh!" She covered her mouth with her hand. "I knew something was wrong. Did your mom and dad call the police?"

Sarah nodded. "They'll be looking today."

"I know they'll find her."

"Thanks," Sarah said. "I got scared last night by myself." She felt herself blush. This was the most personal thing she'd ever said to anyone other than

Carlie. She hoped Kim wouldn't think she was being a baby.

"Oh, I'd be scared, too, if it weren't for my dog."

"Really?" Sarah said. "I wish I had a dog or someone."

Steve Arnold came flying into the room with a shoelace slapping the floor. "Hey, out of my seat, Nomura," he said. Kim got up and shot a smile at Steve. The bell rang and the kids all settled into their seats.

All day, Sarah gazed out the window. She tried to keep her attention focused on the front of the room, but it was no use. Carlie was out there somewhere, not on the blackboard with the sentences Mrs. Lubie was writing. Her teacher glanced toward her several times, but she didn't say anything.

When school finally let out, Mrs. Lubie motioned to her. "Is everything okay?" she asked.

"Everything is fine," Sarah answered. "I think I'm catching a cold is all."

Tell someone, Jesse had said. But Sarah knew she couldn't tell her teacher anything like this.

Mrs. Lubie tilted her head in sympathy. "Well, go home and take some aspirin and a hot bath. And get some sleep. Those eyes look a little red."

"Thanks," Sarah said. "I will." Mrs. Lubie never seemed to consider that Sarah Neville would not be telling the truth. This thought in itself made her feel angry. Why couldn't adults figure things out for themselves?

When Sarah left the school, she immediately spotted Jesse sitting behind the wheel of Lew's old white truck parked near the corner.

He rolled down the window. "Hey, hop in, sister," he called.

Sarah pulled her collar around her ears and ran to the truck. "Did you find out anything?"

"Not yet." Jesse was still wearing his coveralls with a flannel shirt underneath. "I just got the truck. We were real busy this morning."

"I better not go with you," Sarah said. "I should go right home. Carlie could be there already."

Jesse shook his head. "She didn't come back. I've been watching all day. Come on. I might need you."

"Well . . ." If Carlie wasn't home, Sarah wanted to go—anything but sit alone in that bedroom again. Still, if her mother had stayed home, she'd notice if Sarah was late.

"I don't know. How long will it take?"

"Lew thinks I went after a hamburger and shake. I gotta be quick."

Without thinking further, Sarah ran to the opposite side of the truck. The door creaked loudly on its hinges as Jesse pushed it open for her. She reached for his hand and let him hoist her up onto the leathery seat. Scraps of paper, bent playing cards, crushed cigarette packs, a ballpoint pen and an old door handle all lay on the floor on the passenger side. Sarah pushed things around to make room for her feet and settled back.

At the stop signs, Jesse shifted gears beside her. "Maybe we'll spot her bike."

"It's red."

"I know. That should stick out like a sore thumb."

From South Hill, they went north down Grand past the Episcopal cathedral and the ridge of expensive homes with old carriage houses out back. At the bottom of the hill and a few blocks from the Spokane River were The Crescent, Penney's, Woolworth's and other downtown businesses.

Jesse bumped the truck over the train tracks north of the stores and headed for Trent. Everyone knew about Trent. That was where the bums hung out. . . . Then a shadow folded across the truck as they moved under a bridge and went up an alley of crooked bricks and oily-looking puddles.

"Where are we going?" Sarah asked. She already knew the answer. This was where they might find Carlie.

"This was my neighborhood for a while," Jesse said. "Not too pretty, huh?"

Sarah watched out the window, pulling her elbows close to her as if she could protect herself from whatever was out there. She looked for a shoe or a blue coat or a red bike, anything that belonged to Carlie, and at the same time hoped they wouldn't find anything.

They went down one alley and up another. The sound of water rushing along the nearby river hung in the background. They passed garbage cans, stacks of wooden boxes and wads of blankets. In a doorway halfway down the alley stood a group of four kids, one of them a blond girl. Jesse slowed down. As the truck approached, a scar-faced boy turned slightly and looked over his shoulder. He was smaller than the others and wore a black jacket with the collar standing up around his neck.

Hood. That's what kids called boys like him. When he turned to face them, Sarah could see that something was hidden in the front of his jacket. The other boys leaned against the doorjamb, smoking cigarettes.

The girl was skinny and wore a torn sweater underneath a buttonless coat. Yellow hair hung in dirty clumps over her shoulders. She looked pale, but was kind of cute with blood-red lipstick on a pouty mouth. Her eye caught Sarah's as she turned to look into the truck. Sarah looked away.

Jesse stopped the truck and rolled down the window. Instantly, the odor of rotting garbage filled the truck. "Hey, Jackpot, you still living down here?" he called to the kid in the black jacket. Up close he looked no older than twelve or thirteen.

"Hi, Jesse." The boy grinned. "I got responsibilities now." He opened his jacket to show a little brown puppy. The girl reached over and patted its head. Then one of the other boys reached out and patted the puppy, too, as if they all owned it jointly.

"What are you doing here with those wheels?" one of the smokers asked, flipping his cigarette butt into the alley. "How about taking us for a ride?"

"Can't," Jesse said. "We're looking for someone. Someone new last night—a girl."

"Not here," the kid said.

"She might be on a red bike, an old boys' bike."

With this the kids all exchanged guilty looks, and Sarah felt the blood drain from her face.

thirteen

JESSE PUSHED OPEN his door and stepped out, keeping one foot inside the truck. "Okay, who's seen the bike?"

"Maybe we seen something," the other smoker admitted, "but there wasn't any girl."

Sarah felt a wave of relief. "There could be lots of red bikes, couldn't there, Jesse?"

"Not down here. A bike would be a real find."

Jackpot played nervously with the puppy's ears.

"So who was on it?" Jesse pursued.

"All of us took turns," Jackpot told him. "It was just a piece of junk, all bent up. Then some big guy took off on it."

The girl glared into the truck at Sarah. "What's so special about this piece of lace? She from a rich family or something?"

Lace? Was she talking about Carlie? Sarah glared back.

"Look, she's a friend of mine," Jesse said, fitting

himself back into the truck. "And I don't want anything to happen to her if she shows up down here, okay?"

"What could happen here?" the girl said with a snide laugh. "This hole's as cozy as any fancy hotel."

"She's not exactly smart about some things, you know what I mean?"

"Well, isn't that a shame?" She shifted her weight so her hip stuck out.

Ignoring her, Jesse reached into his pocket. "Here are a couple of dimes for the phone." He handed them to Jackpot. "You can call me at Lew's 66 up on the hill if you hear anything." He pulled the door shut. "I gotta go. See ya." Then he waved and drove slowly out of the alley.

Sarah caught the kids' reflections in the rearview mirror. They were all watching them leave as if this visit were the most interesting thing that had happened all day.

She remained quiet until Jesse had pulled into traffic again. "Do you think they'll call?"

"Probably not. They'll buy coffee."

Sarah shuddered. It was as if they weren't even kids. "That one boy looks like a seventh grader."

"That's about right—not that he ever goes to school," Jesse said. "Look, these kids are not just delinquents, you know. Some of them have good reasons for being down here."

"I know that." Sarah felt suddenly embarrassed

for sounding so naïve. Did Jesse have a good reason? she wondered. And did it even matter? Carlie had said his father had kicked him out, but that didn't explain everything. She would ask him someday, but not now. "Shouldn't we look for the bike?" she asked. "Maybe it isn't even hers."

"I'll swing through the area, then I've got to get Lew's truck back like I promised."

Jesse drove through half a dozen alleys. Deep pot-holes and buckled stretches of brick slowed them to a crawl as they passed rows of garbage cans. Sarah forced her eyes into every corner, searching for anything red.

When they found nothing, Jesse left the alleys and went back out to Trent, then up to Main Street, where they turned right. After several stoplights he turned into a gravel driveway next to an insurance agency. The drive led to an old white house.

"Wait here. This is the home. I'll ask if she's been here."

Jesse dashed up onto the porch while Sarah checked the outside from the truck. The place looked like any ordinary, run-down house with peeling paint and a lawn that was mostly weeds and dirt. There were no signs out front saying it was a place for boys, so it didn't seem likely that Carlie could find her way here alone.

Jesse dashed back out, jumping off the edge of the porch. "Shoot!" he said. "I kind of thought . . . but, no sign of her here, either." He got back into the truck, then sat for a minute rubbing his chin, crossing and uncrossing his arms and thumping the steering wheel. Like Sarah, he seemed angry and worried at the same time. Finally, he shoved the truck into gear and they were off again.

"Well, time's up," Jesse said. "If she's not home when we get back, she's a missing person officially. They'll find her quick enough."

"You think so?" If only it were true. Sarah glanced toward the river, but would not let her mind go into the dark water. "How long did it take them to find you?"

Jesse stopped at a light. "A while, but then, I knew how to be cagey."

They rode on for a while in silence. Tears welled again in Sarah's eyes. Carlie would never just give her bike to anyone. They would have to take it from her. "Do you think someone, you know . . ."

"I hope not," Jesse said. "We can't think that way."

A few minutes later, he pulled in at an A&W drive-in. "I guess I'd better show up with a hamburger wrapper. How about it? I got a couple of bucks."

"Sure, that would be nice." Sarah's stomach felt full of worry, but she was hungry. She was always hungry, it seemed. Then something unsettling occurred to her: Carlie was the one who should be here with Jesse, not her. Carlie's date with Jesse had started all the trouble in the first place.

A girl in a tight blue uniform came to the window and took their order. In spite of the worry, Sarah sat up straight, hoping she looked older than twelve. She checked down the line of other cars, mostly high school kids laughing and drinking root beers. Were any of these kids from Carlie's school? she wondered. Did they know she was missing?

In just a few minutes, the girl returned with a large white bag. Jesse gave her some money and took the bag, which he handed to Sarah. Through the paper she could feel the warmth of the hamburgers and the cold of the big paper cups that held the root beer. The aroma of french fries filled the truck.

Sarah handed Jesse a burger, then pushed a straw into one of the drinks and balanced it between her knees. She ate too fast, thinking she had never had such a wonderful meal, and Carlie was missing the whole thing!

Later, when they passed the high school, Sarah leaned forward to scan the steps and the bushes and the walkways. School had let out more than an hour ago now, and no one was around. "We've been gone a long time."

"I'll drop you off by your garage," Jesse said. "If you hear anything new, come out to the alley and let me know, okay?"

"I will," Sarah said. She looked down Sherman, hoping something would be different, as if Carlie's presence might show in the trees or the air outside the house.

"Maybe she didn't go downtown," Sarah said. "Maybe she went someplace else, like a church or something. Unless she's already home."

"Yeah, maybe." Jesse stopped on the far side of the Nevilles' garage. "Let me know. I gotta get back to work."

"Okay, bye." Sarah was not looking at him, but at the house. "Thanks, Jesse." She jumped out and ran up the walk. Across the yard and in through the back porch, she watched for signs all the way— Carlie's jacket on the hook or the pillowcase she'd packed.

The kitchen lights were on. Sarah sniffed. Pie! Suddenly, hope leapt into her chest.

"Where've you been?" Her mother materialized from the living room wearing a brown dress with a full skirt and big white buttons down the front. A suit would mean she'd been to work—this meant something else, that she was dressed up for some other reason.

Sarah ignored the angry tone. "Is she home?"

"Tt! Not hardly. Why are you so late?"

Sarah felt herself sag. "I stayed after to finish my math."

"You've been eating something."

"Mrs. Lubie brought cookies," Sarah lied. She hoped her ride with Jesse didn't show on her face.

The whole thing seemed unreal now anyway, not part of her life in the bedroom upstairs.

"Well, I'm glad I don't have to put up with two of you missing. This has been unbearable. The police have been here, and your father is acting like a mad fool."

"What'd the police say?"

"Nothing. That selfish thing is holing up somewhere, if you ask me. She's doing this to me on purpose. She'll probably sashay in when she's good and ready."

Sarah had no resonse to this. She could see that her mother wanted her to side against Carlie. "It smells good in here," she said.

"Apple cobbler." Her mother brightened. "And spareribs. We may as well have a decent meal."

"Oh." It wasn't just a decent meal, it was *special.* The police had been here, Dad was upset, Sarah had been late and everything was exciting. This was the way her mother had acted one time when the insurance man came to visit, too. She had dressed up and baked coffee cake. Sarah wasn't fooled. Could her mother's life be so boring that anything out of the ordinary, even if it was bad, was a reason to celebrate?

Sarah looked away. She didn't want to be any part of this. And mixed into her understanding was something else she could not quite get hold of. It was as if her mother wanted to seem like a different person, even to herself. Just in case. In case Carlie never came back. In case she got mad enough to use her bathrobe strap or the hanger again. Then, no matter what happened, she could remember the time she'd made a special dinner and dressed up so nice.

Sarah turned and ran up the stairs, her hamburger still heavy in her stomach. If only she'd gone with Carlie, she wouldn't have to be here in the middle of all this craziness. Maybe Carlie was right and this family could never be just normal. Before she reached the top of the stairs, she craned her neck to see through the railing into their room. She knew it was impossible, yet she hoped Carlie would be sitting there quietly, waiting to surprise her.

But everything was exactly as Sarah had left it that morning: the unmade beds, the socks on the floor, the books, the papers. She stood between the beds, hugging herself, trying to feel warm. It was going on two days now. Where had Carlie slept? What had she eaten? Sarah swallowed a sob before it could bellow up through her throat. If she gave in to it now, she'd never be able to stop crying.

When the family of three was seated in the dining room for their special dinner, Sarah peered up through her eyelashes at her parents. All puffy and red faced, Dad looked agitated, like he might come loose from his chair and go flying around the room. Her mother kept her eyebrows high and breathed deeply as if she were trying to prove that she wasn't bothered a bit by Carlie's absence.

It occurred to Sarah after a few minutes that in some ways her mother had been right: Carlie was being selfish to make everyone act so strange. Their father kept dropping his forehead into his hand and saying over and over, "Why in the world would she do something like this?"

Because nobody really wants her . . . except me.

"They'll check the bus and train stations," he said. "If she's left town, we should have an answer by tonight, unless she's been the victim of foul play. Why in the world would she do something like this?"

"She'll be home soon enough," her mother said. "Tt! Who knows what kind of story she'll concoct when they find her?"

Sarah looked up from her plate, glancing at her mother, then at her father, who had stopped chewing. Sometimes for brief moments like this, Sarah wondered if her father understood more than he pretended. But if he did, why didn't he do something?

"Did you tell them she was on her bike?" Sarah asked.

Dad looked shocked. "She was on her bike?" He turned toward her mother. "Did you tell them that? I didn't know she was on her bike! That's important."

"Of course I did," she said with a sneer. "I'm sure she got tired of pumping that thing in a hurry. Tt!"

There it was again, that sound her mother always

made. The sound that Sarah had always understood as something ugly, even though her mother had never explained what it meant. She took a deep, quivery breath and her chin began to wobble. She'd had enough for two days. She couldn't take much more of this.

"Now what?" her mother asked. "You're not going to cry, are you?"

Sarah squeezed her eyes shut. "No."

"I hope not. Your face looks ridiculous all scrunched up like that. Straighten up and eat your dinner."

"I *am* eating!" *Leave me alone. Carlie is my sister and I can act any way I want.*

When the telephone rang, Dad's chair nearly tipped over as he got up to answer it.

"Yes, she's right here," Dad said. "No, I'm afraid not. Not yet. That's very kind of you. I suppose my wife would know more about that. Why don't you talk to her?"

"Who?" her mother mouthed as the brown dress swished past Dad on the way to the telephone.

"A Mrs. Nomura," Dad whispered.

Her mother looked surprised. Sarah straightened. "Nomura? I know a girl with that name." But it sounded like they were talking about Carlie. What would Kim's mom know about Carlie?

When her mother hung up and returned to the table, she said, "Why didn't you tell us you had a friend who is Japanese?"

"I don't know." She hadn't told her mother she had any friends at all, Japanese or otherwise. Besides, she hadn't thought it mattered.

"You know what they did at Pearl Harbor, don't you?"

Dad rubbed his forehead. "Margaret, the girl's only twelve; she wasn't responsible for what happened in the war."

"What did you tell them about us?"

Sarah stared up at her mother's face. What had she told Kim? She tried to remember the words. She hadn't said much, just that Carlie had left.

"Well, the Nomuras apparently are feeling sorry for you. They want you to come spend the night."

"I can't!" Sarah put in quickly. "I have to be here when Carlie comes back."

"Well, don't hold your breath. If you ask me, we won't see her for days."

Dad winced. Sarah's chest felt like it would cave in with the pain of it all. How could anyone say something like that right out loud, as if it might be true?

"Teenagers are so self-centered," her mother added. "Maybe it's a good idea. I could use some peace and quiet after..." Her voice cracked. "...the day I've had."

Dad stood up and put his arm around her shoulder. "It's okay, Margaret. It's okay." Then sharply to

Sarah, "Go call your friend." He sounded like he was just barely hanging on himself.

Sarah clenched her teeth, feeling guilty again for existing. She scraped her chair back and stood up. Carlie was the only one who didn't have to listen to this. Lucky Carlie.

Sarah went to the phone, feeling their eyes on her back. By now she knew Kim's number by heart, but she pretended to check the pad where her mother had written it down and dialed. Kim herself answered.

"Hi. This is Sarah."

"Oh, Sarah. Don't be mad at me," Kim said in her high, sweet voice. "I just couldn't bear to think of you alone there without your sister, being scared all night, when I have an extra bed and a dog here."

Sarah felt herself go soft. Tears welled again in her eyes. "Thanks," was all she could think to say.

Her mother stood in the doorway. "Now, you stay away from Mrs. Nomura. She doesn't want a kid hanging around, bending her ear all night long. I'm sure they've got plenty of problems of their own without wallowing in ours too."

"I won't bother her," Sarah said.

"You'll have a good time," Dad assured her. "Ready?"

As her father drove her to the Nomuras' house, Sarah could tell he was checking everywhere for Carlie or her bike. He slowed down at the alleys and dark driveways and seemed to be looking in the windows wherever the drapes weren't closed.

It was dark again and even colder than last night. Frost had already settled on the lawns. Carlie must be good and scared by now.

In spite of everything, though, Sarah felt relieved that she wouldn't have to lie awake for hours tonight, wondering about rats or listening at the grate to her parents talk about her sister.

"Promise you'll call?" Sarah asked as she got out of the truck.

"I promise," Dad said. He got out, too, and walked to the door with her. "With a little luck, we'll have her back tonight. Your mother's awfully upset."

Sarah didn't answer. She hugged her pillow to her. Inside the pillowcase she had stuffed her nightgown and toothbrush wrapped in toilet paper. Under the porch light, she took a deep breath while her father rang the bell. I shouldn't be here, she thought. I need to be home.

Inside, something bounded down the stairs and gallumped across the floor to the door, where it stood and barked. Sarah braced herself for the door to open. When it did, Kim and her mother stood with the dog between them. It was woolly and black and waist high to Mrs. Nomura.

"Come in!" Kim squealed. She grabbed Sarah's arm and pulled her inside. The dog licked her fingers as she moved past him, and Sarah patted his big curly head.

"Out of the way, Boo," Mrs. Nomura said, pulling on the dog's collar. The woman had a round face and smiling eyes, just like Kim. "How about introductions, Kimmie?"

"Oh, sorry." Kim covered her mouth and giggled.

Kim made introductions, then Sarah did the same, relieved when her father smiled at Mrs. Nomura. In a moment a short, bulky man came to the door, too.

"Nice to meet you," he said in a big voice. "I'm Jim Nomura." He shook Dad's hand. "We're awfully sorry about your daughter. Any news?"

"Not yet, but the police are hoping to clear it up quickly."

"Well, don't you worry one bit about Sarah," Mrs. Nomura said. "We'll take good care of her."

"Thanks," Dad said. "Like I said, we're hoping to resolve this right away. I'm sure we will. How far can a girl get on a bicycle, huh?" He turned to Sarah and touched her elbow lightly. "You be polite," he said, and then he was gone.

Sarah stood uneasily in the doorway, her hand resting on Boo's head. She had never stayed at anyone else's house before, not once. She just hoped she'd get through it somehow and that she and Kim would still be friends afterward.

fourteen

SARAH WALKED AWKWARDLY into Kim's living room. Boo settled down on the stairs with his chin resting on his big paws.

"He's kind of big, but he won't hurt you," Kim said.

"I like dogs," Sarah said. "What kind is he?"

Mr. Nomura answered, "He's a standard poodle, but don't tell him. He'll want to get clipped like the others."

Sarah laughed. Boo was woolly all over, like a tall black lamb. She smiled at him and he seemed to smile back, with his mouth open and his teeth showing.

The living room looked friendly, but strange at the same time. This didn't smell like her house; this house smelled like . . . candle wax, or something else Sarah couldn't identify. In the corner stood a sewing machine with fancy black legs. Behind it on a curtain rod hung an unhemmed girl's dress of red and blue plaid with a rounded white collar. Kim's dress. A stab of envy caught Sarah by surprise.

"This is going to be so much fun," Kim said, clutching Sarah's arm. "I have something to show you in my room."

Mr. Nomura chuckled. "Keep it down to a dull roar, you two."

Boo came to attention and followed Kim as she scrambled up the stairs. Sarah walked politely behind them, taking in every detail of the house.

A strip of flowered carpet folded its way up the stairs with threads showing bare in the middle. Sarah stopped halfway up to look at photographs in carved frames on the wall. Except for one old fashioned–looking wedding picture, the photos were all of Japanese people huddling around a little girl. Sarah could tell it was Kim at different ages.

On a little shelf at the top of the stairs sat the most beautiful doll Sarah had ever seen. With a chalk-white face and mound of black hair, she stood in a glass box in a red-and-orange kimono. Draped over her shoulder was a sprig of lavender flowers. Sarah stopped to look at it, then hurried after Kim.

Pushing through the doorway with Boo, Sarah saw that Kim's bedroom was a clutter of interesting things. A lamp cast a soft light on the floor where a tray of nail polish bottles and cotton balls sat on a fringed, pink rug. Worn butterfly-patterned bed-spreads in pale pink and lavender covered each of the two twin beds.

A round table between the beds was just big enough for a lamp and several magazines—movie magazines and *Seventeen*. The tablecloth in the same fabric as the bedspreads draped all the way to the floor. And Kim had her own record player. The turquoise box sat open on the floor at the foot of her bed, and records in their square envelopes littered the rug.

Sarah would have to tell Carlie about this amazing bedroom—if she ever saw her again. Standing uncertainly just inside the room, she clutched her pillow, twisting the case in her fist. She had not thought about her shoulder all day, but now it ached.

Kim stood watching her. "You look nervous," she said. "Are you worried about your sister?"

Sarah nodded. "Not just that."

"What?"

"Well . . ." Sarah studied the friendly face across the room. "I don't stay overnight with friends all that often."

Kim smiled. "Oh, me neither."

"Actually . . . I've *never* done it before," Sarah confessed.

"Really?" Kim's eyes widened as if she couldn't believe it. "Well, good! Then I can teach you how to do an overnight. First, you pick which bed you want."

"I might not be staying all night," Sarah warned

her, "not if Carlie comes home."

"That's okay. My dad said he'd take you home anytime."

"Thanks," Sarah said, relaxing a little. "Where do you usually sleep?"

"Well, I trade off," she said. "Sometimes I sleep over here . . ." She leapt onto the bed nearest the window, messing up the bedspread. Then she jumped down and leapt onto the other bed. "And sometimes I sleep here." She landed on the floor between the two beds with her arms flung wide. "Okay, you pick."

Sarah watched Kim in amazement. At her house, jumping on beds would make noise downstairs, so she and Carlie never did it. *Was this a dull roar?* she wondered.

Sarah pointed to the bed on the left, in the same position as her bed at home. She felt sure she wouldn't be able to sleep otherwise. "If you don't mind, I'll take this one."

"Okay," Kim said. "Now for a surprise." She stood with her hand to her mouth as if she were stifling a giggle. "Look under your pillow."

Sarah laughed. "How did you know which bed I would pick?" She lifted the pillow, and there on the sheet was a shiny book with a spaceship on the front. "David Henley! *Amalthean Summer*!"

Kim pulled an identical book out from under her own pillow and held it up for her to see. "I just got them tonight at the main library. They're brand new."

Sarah hugged her copy to her. "Oh, I can't wait to read it." She was aware that her face had slid into a smile, but now she pulled it back again. She didn't want to be like her mother and act like things were happier without Carlie. She looked anxiously toward the door. "Do you think we can hear the telephone from here?"

"Oh, it's plenty loud." Kim's face grew serious. "My mom said maybe you'd get your mind off things if you came over here."

"Thanks. I'll try," Sarah promised. She took a breath and let it out again, then arranged her pillow on the bed and propped David Henley on top.

Kim copied her, putting her book on top of her pillow. "Okay, the next thing you do on an overnight is fix something to eat. Let's go make some popcorn."

Boo sprang to his feet as if he knew the word "popcorn." Then all three of them trotted back down the stairs.

Kim flipped on the light in a yellow kitchen where pretty plates hung on the walls like pictures. A table and two cushioned benches fit exactly into a little nook. Sarah wondered if an only child ate there alone or if she ate in the dining room with her parents.

She stood nervously near the sink while Kim got

a tall can of popcorn out of the cupboard and poured a little puddle of oil into a pan. Her parents, who were reading in the living room, didn't seem to mind what the girls were doing.

Soon the kitchen smelled wonderful. Kim dumped half the popcorn into a bowl and got two bottles of Coca-Cola out of the refrigerator, handing one to Sarah. Wet and cold, not lukewarm like the bottles she and Carlie stole from the back porch.

Kim took the rest of the popcorn in to her parents.

"Popcorn for your ol' pop," her dad joked. "Thanks, sweetheart."

Sweetheart.

Boo danced around next to Sarah on the tile floor, his toenails clicking. "Can he have some?" she asked when Kim returned.

"He loves popcorn. But I'm warning you, he'll want all of it."

Sarah dropped one piece, then stood out of Boo's way as he chased it around on the floor.

Kim handed the bowl to Sarah. "Come on, Boo." They all trooped back upstairs, and Sarah felt herself relax in the warmth of Kim's room.

"We should go shopping at The Crescent some-time," Kim said. "They have the best records."

"I know," Sarah said, even though she didn't. The girls sat cross-legged on the floor between the beds with the bowl in the middle and listened to one record after another. Eddie Fisher, Rosemary Clooney, Johnnie Ray. They bumped their shoulders in time with the music. Sarah smiled.

Boo sat politely, watching them eat popcorn as if it were a Ping-Pong match. He turned first toward Kim, then toward Sarah. Each time he looked at Sarah, she handed him a piece. After a while he lay down next to her with his big head on her leg.

"Told you so," Kim said.

"I like him." Sarah patted his warm wool and rubbed his ears.

When the phone rang downstairs, Sarah jumped. "That could be my dad!"

Kim sprang to the door and listened. "No, it's my grandma. She calls all the time." She sat down again. "Why don't we pretend we're sisters, just for tonight? We could do whatever you and Carlie do together."

Sarah considered this. She couldn't tell Kim that she and Carlie listened to their parents at the grate and ate food they kept in the wall. Or that they got into the bathtub together to make it quicker. Kim wouldn't understand any of it.

Then she thought of something. "There is this one thing we do that's kind of fun," Sarah said. "But it's for after we get into bed."

Kim pulled in her shoulders and laughed. "Okay," she said. "Let's put on our nightgowns right now." She led Sarah down the hall and turned on the light in a pale green-and-white bathroom. "You first."

The room was clean and warm, with no door on the other side to worry about like at her house. On a shelf were things that belonged to Kim: a small bottle of perfume with a pink bow painted on the front, barrettes with plastic flowers attached, and a basket that held rings and bracelets.

Sarah looked at her white face in the mirror. Did she really want to play Draw-in-the-Dark without Carlie? Maybe it would be okay this once. She brushed her teeth quickly and put on her old nightgown, arranging it carefully to cover her bruise.

A few minutes later, she and Kim stood in the middle of the bedroom together. Kim's nightgown was flannel with pink polka dots and still looked bright and new. If she noticed the difference, though, she didn't say anything.

"Okay, ready?" Sarah said. "We need some tablet paper and pencils to play the game."

Kim took some paper out of a drawer, and the girls got into their beds, each with a magazine to draw against.

Sarah fluffed the cool sheets over her knees, releasing a puff of sweet detergent fragrance. "Now, what you do is fold the paper like this." Sarah showed Kim how to do it. "Then we think up pictures to draw in the squares."

Kim smiled as if she were already having fun.

"But we have to draw the pictures in the dark," Sarah said, "so they turn out pretty funny."

"In the dark? You're kidding." Giggling, Kim got up and turned out the light, then got back into her bed.

"Feel along the creases with your fingers. That way you can tell which square you're drawing in," Sarah said. "Okay, you go first. What do you want to draw?"

"How about Boo with a bowl of popcorn? Is that too hard?"

"No, no, that's a good one." Both girls laughed and went to work. When it was Sarah's turn, she said, "Let's draw us reading books."

Soon they had filled both sides of their papers. When they were finished, Kim jumped out of bed and sprang toward the wall.

"Okay, let's see what we drew," she said, flicking on the light.

Sarah blinked. She felt her mouth open.

"What's the matter?" Kim asked.

"Nothing." This wasn't the way the game was played! "It's just that Carlie and I never look until the next day."

"You don't? How come?"

Because getting out of bed makes noise down-stairs—a dull roar, Sarah thought. Because our mother would come charging upstairs if she saw light through the grate. "Because . . . well, it's just more fun to play in the dark."

"Oh, okay. Yeah. I see what you mean." Kim flipped the light off again, but Sarah could tell she didn't really understand.

"Do you ever use flashlights?" Kim asked.

"No." For some reason Sarah had never thought of that. There were several flashlights in the kitchen drawer at home. If she and Carlie stole bread, they could certainly sneak a flashlight, too.

Kim's bed creaked as she got back in. Boo scratched, then settled again. "I know what we can do next. Let's trade secrets," Kim suggested.

"Secrets?"

"It's fun."

"I don't know," Sarah hesitated. *No one* knew anything about her except Carlie, and now Jesse. It would seem almost wrong to tell any real secrets. "Do you have one?"

Kim laughed. "I have a big one." After a long pause and another burst of giggles, she said, "But you have to swear you won't tell."

"I swear."

"Well . . . , I think Steve Arnold is really cute."

Sarah's hand went to her mouth. "Steve Arnold! He's so skinny!" She threw her head back and laughed, too. "He's not half as cute as David Henley."

"Yeah, but at least he's real."

Waves of laughter grew louder and louder. Sarah glanced at the door several times, expecting it to fly open, but no one came running upstairs to tell them to be quiet.

"Okay, your turn," Kim said. "What's your secret?" She didn't seem worried about the noise.

Sarah didn't have any funny secrets like Kim did, but then something did come to her. "Well . . . I went out for hamburgers with a boy today."

Kim gasped. "Are you serious? With who? How old is he?"

"He's seventeen and his name is Jesse. We had hamburgers, french fries and root beer, and he paid for everything."

"Gosh!" Kim said, as if she were truly amazed. "That's a real *date*."

Sarah smiled. "Yeah, I guess it was."

"How do you know him?"

"Well," Sarah said, feeling pleased with herself, "he's sort of my sister's boyfriend. We went downtown looking for her. Jesse thought maybe she had gone to this house for juvenile delinquents."

"Really?"

"Yeah. We saw this girl with dirty hair and a boy with a terrible scar. It was really creepy. They may have seen Carlie's bike."

"Oh, my gosh!" Kim exclaimed. "That's a good clue." Then she added, "I'd be too scared to run away. Why do you think she did it?"

"It's sort of complicated. You might not understand."

"Maybe I would," Kim begged.

"Well, it's not the awful kinds of things you read about. But our mother doesn't like . . ." She started to say "us," but instead she said, "Carlie." That her mother didn't like her, either, seemed far too personal.

"She doesn't like her? How do you know?"

"I just know." This was hard to explain. "She calls her names," Sarah said simply.

"That's terrible!"

Then Sarah told Kim about the bath, the bottle, the dress and the hanger, and some other things that had happened a long time ago. In a way she wished she could see her friend's face, but maybe it was easier to tell secrets in the dark.

A moment of silence followed, then Kim said, "No wonder your sister ran away. Gee, I try on my mother's dresses all the time. She lets me."

"Remember, you promised not to tell," Sarah warned. "Not even your parents."

"Don't worry. I won't tell," Kim said. "But you should." She sounded angry. "You should call your dad right now and explain everything. I bet he'll do something."

"No," Sarah said, "he doesn't care." It all sounded so simple when Kim said it. But it wasn't as if she and Carlie lived in the middle of photographs with people huddled around like Kim did. "Anyway, it's not like our mother is breaking the law."

"Well, maybe not, but . . . I don't think I like her."

Silence again, except for Boo biting at his paw.

"It's not everything," Sarah added. "We have fun in our bedroom."

"Well . . ."

"And we have *agendas*," Sarah said. She thought about the bubble bath they had taken with the laundry soap and the teacups that fell off the roof, how they had laughed. She thought about bringing Carlie the note from Jesse. It seemed like a hundred years ago now.

She slid down into her covers, wishing once again that she were home. The room grew quiet. Boo lay sleeping, breathing and sighing on the floor between the beds.

Sarah turned onto her side, looking through the darkness toward Kim. Maybe she shouldn't have told so much. What would her friend think of her tomorrow or next year? What if they weren't friends forever? Her mother would be furious if she found out Sarah had told things about the family.

But worse than that, Carlie was no longer the only person to know these things. Sarah wasn't sure she liked that, words swirling around in the air to be plucked by anyone. A sense of fear clutched at her, as if she had nowhere to hide from the knowing. She felt exposed and cold in this unfamiliar bedroom.

Sarah let her arm dangle over the side of the bed

where she could touch Boo's head. He rose up and licked her fingers.

Sarah patted the bed. "Come on," she whispered. With surprising grace, Boo jumped up onto the bed, turned around twice and flopped down next to her, his collar jingling. Sarah hugged him around the middle and pulled his warm woolly back against her face.

"You shouldn't encourage him," Kim said, breaking the silence. "He'll wiggle around until he gets the whole bed."

Sarah laughed, but tears started to form in the corners of her eyes. It felt so good to have something to hug, something alive and warm. "He's okay, I don't mind." Boo sighed and shifted a little.

A while later, Sarah had just closed her eyes and settled on her pillow when the telephone rang out downstairs. She sat up and strained to listen. In the dimness, she saw Kim rise up on her elbows. Boo lifted his big head.

Sarah heard a muffled voice, then footsteps on the stairs. Her heart pounded. She knew what was coming. In a moment, there was a soft knock on the door.

"Sarah," Mrs. Nomura called. "It's for you, honey. It's your dad."

fifteen

KIM AND BOO followed Sarah out of the room and down the stairs where Mrs. Nomura handed her the receiver.

Boo pressed himself against her knee. "Dad?"

"The police have found your sister's bike." Her father sounded out of breath. "They want to ask you some questions. Right away."

"What about Carlie?" Sarah saw pictures of the kids in the alley and the mounds of blankets, of Carlie's red bike. "What about her clothes and the pillowcase?"

Kim stood watching Sarah's face.

"Get your things together," Dad said without answering. "I'll be there in ten minutes to pick you up." His voice sounded far away and cold.

"I can come home with Mr. Nomura. He said he'd bring me."

Her father sounded relieved. A few minutes later, the girls were riding in the back of the Nomuras' car, with their arms interlocked.

Kim leaned close. "Finding her bike doesn't mean anything's happened to her."

"I know, but now I'm really scared. I should have stopped her somehow."

They turned the corner sharply at Thirty-eighth. Sarah looked expectantly down the street to Sherman, where a police car was parked in front of the house with its lights flashing. Even though she had known it would be there, her stomach knotted at the sight. She reached for the door handle just as Mr. Nomura stopped in front of the house.

Sarah got out without waiting for Kim and hurried past the police car. The flashing lights illuminated Carlie's bike propped against the porch, as if her sister had only forgotten to put it in the garage.

Sarah felt Kim and Mr. Nomura behind her as she rounded the side of the house. It occurred to her to tell them to go in through the front door—it was only she and Carlie who weren't allowed—but she said nothing and went in through the screened back porch. Kim and her dad followed her in.

Two policemen dominated the center of the living room, big and dark blue, with belts slung around their waists. Sarah felt her mouth open. She had never seen a policeman this close before. Her eyes focused on the guns at their sides, dull black and heavy looking, cased in leather holsters.

One of them, a blond man with a boy's face,

stood writing something in a notebook. The other one looked old, her father's age.

Her mother sat in Dad's chair with her face in her hands. Was she crying? An unsmoked cigarette lay in an ashtray at her elbow.

"Sarah . . ." Dad stepped forward from behind the chair. "Here's her sister."

Both officers turned toward her, but before they could say anything, her mother straightened abruptly and pulled in a long breath. "Why is she doing this to me?"

"We're seeing a lot of runaways this year, ma'am," the older policeman said. "You know how it is—nothing's exciting enough for kids these days."

Sarah glared at him. He didn't even know Carlie; how could he think such things? Then she noticed something clipped to the top of his notebook—it looked like Carlie's note from Jesse. Did this mean the police had been searching their bedroom? Their private place?

"Tell them everything," her father instructed her.

She couldn't tell them everything, not here in the living room in front of everyone.

"My name's Thomas," the younger one said. He sounded nicer than the other one. "This is Officer Grimes. You're Sarah Neville, is that right?"

Sarah nodded.

"Carlisle seems to know a fellow named Jesse." He held his pen ready to write. "Do you know

194

anything about him?"

Sarah glanced at Kim. "Yes, I know him."

Her mother's head jerked upward. "I knew it."

"He's just a boy who works at the gas station," Sarah added.

"The Phillips 66 station across the alley?" Thomas wrote on his pad.

"Yes, but Jesse didn't do anything. He *didn't*." Sarah felt her legs go weak. This was worse than Carlie could have imagined.

"It's okay, we just want to talk to him. He might be able to tell us something."

"Would you mind coming outside and taking a look at this bike?" Grimes asked.

"I don't want to look. I know it's hers."

"Sarah, please," her mother whimpered.

"Just to be sure," Grimes said. "Your folks weren't positive."

Sarah glanced at her father, who seemed focused on a spot on the floor. Carlie had had that red boys' bike forever. Dad had paid three dollars for it used. How could they not know it was hers? She moved past Kim and stepped out onto the porch with both policemen.

Carlie's bike leaned against the house, below the yellow porch light. Now Sarah could see that one tire was flat and the front fender was bent as if it had hit something. Mud stuck to the spokes.

She stared at the handlebars where Carlie had

slung the pillowcase, except the pillowcase wasn't there now. "That's her bike," she whispered and looked away.

Grimes then went to the edge of the front porch and jumped off, his gear slapping at his sides. With a fat stick that had been hanging from his belt, he poked at the bushes, then shined a bright flashlight around the side yard.

"You kids," he said, "getting your folks all upset. A week or two in Juvie ought to cool her off."

"Carlie doesn't need to *cool off*. She's not like that. You just don't know." She didn't like Grimes. He acted like he expected to catch Carlie playing hide-and-seek, crouched next to the house.

"Hey, look," Thomas said. "I think we'll have your sister back to you in no time."

"Really?" If only she could believe that.

"Really. Looks to me like she just got mad and took off. She probably dumped the bike and went to hide out somewhere for a day or two."

"She was really mad," Sarah said.

"I kind of figured that."

Sarah took a deep breath and puffed it out again. Carlie really could be hiding somewhere, waiting for a chance to come home. "Where did you find her bike?" she asked.

"Someone tried to sell it at a used bicycle shop. No name." Thomas looked down at his notebook again. "How can I get in touch with this Jesse? Do you know where he lives?"

"Not exactly." Sarah thought of Jesse in his little room at the gas station. He was probably there this very minute. She'd never actually seen the room, though, so she wasn't really lying.

"We'll check at the gas station tomorrow when they open," Thomas said. He was writing things down again. "What about other friends?"

"Just me," Sarah said. She knew they probably didn't believe her. Most kids had a regular crowd of their own. He asked her some more questions about kids they might know from church or clubs or the neighborhood. He also asked for a list of the things Carlie had packed into the pillowcase.

Inside the house again, Grimes talked for five minutes about all the problems juvenile delinquents were causing these days, how in his day kids had chores to do, and how television and modern conveniences were spoiling society. Sarah's mother kept nodding in agreement, like a toy duck with a spring in its neck.

Thomas said, "Look, I know you're all upset. You might think of something else later. If you do, give us a jingle, okay?" Then both of them left through the front door. Sarah heard a scrape of rubber and metal as they took Carlie's bike down the steps. The sound seemed lonely, as though they were taking away a part of Carlie herself.

"Well," Mr. Nomura said when the police were

gone, "we'd better get going. You folks must be worn out. We'd be glad to help in any way we can."

"Thanks," Dad said. "We are a little tired. You're not seeing us at our best. It's just that . . ."

"I know," Mr. Nomura said. "I hope you don't blame yourselves; this could happen to anyone."

Anyone? Who had this happened to? Sarah wondered. Carlie? Her parents? Or was this something that had happened to Sarah? That's the way it had felt ever since she watched Carlie push off from the curb. Someday she would tell someone, *When I was twelve, my sister ran away, and I was never happy again.*

As they were leaving, Mr. Nomura patted Sarah's shoulder. "You come back as soon as you can, okay?"

"Okay," Sarah said. "I will."

"Bye." Kim squeezed her hand. "Are you going to school tomorrow?"

"I don't know." Sarah shot a look at her parents. They both looked back at her blankly, as if this were too complex to consider right now.

"Well, I'll call right after school, I promise," Kim said.

The Nomuras left and Sarah stood in the living room, wondering what to do next. The house seemed colder and emptier than ever before. She looked at her mother, who sat stony eyed in the chair. Why was she acting this way, Sarah wondered, when she didn't even care about Carlie?

"Can I go upstairs now?" she asked.

No one spoke or changed positions. Dad stood with his hands pushed into his pants pockets. It was as if he, too, were waiting for permission to move.

"It's that kid," her mother said. "He's done something to her, I just know it."

Sarah snapped toward her mother, surprised that she would make up such a story when both of them knew what had really happened.

"I'd like to know why I wasn't told about this kid." Her eyes narrowed, and it occurred to Sarah that she was glad there was a place to put all her anger, now that no one would let her be angry with Carlie anymore.

Sarah didn't speak. How could she answer something like that? *Carlie ran off and got married. We had a beautiful wedding behind the gas station, and now they're on their way to California.* She may as well answer a lie with another lie. It had been years since Sarah had told her mother the truth about much of anything, and she liked it that way, keeping even the smallest secrets to herself.

Finally, her mother turned her head aside. "Tt! I know you're not going to tell me anything."

"Let it go, Margaret," Dad said.

Sarah went back through the kitchen, where she picked up her pillow and the things she had taken to Kim's, then started up the stairs to their room.

She had gone up no more than three steps when she sensed that something was wrong. A slight feeling—in the dust motes or in the walls—made her stiffen and climb the rest of the flight more slowly.

She sniffed, testing the air. Violets! Violets and cigarette smoke. The faint smell hung in the stairwell around her. Her mother had been up here.

Sarah peered up through the railing, anger clamping her stomach tight. The beds had been made, and Carlie's quilt was back on her bed. Their pictures were gone from the walls. Nothing lay on the floor except a neat stack of doll dishes. She stepped up into the room and strode over to the chimney.

Her mother had come into their bedroom and cleaned up. For the police. They had all been in here, looking for things.

She went to Carlie's bed and flipped back the pillow. The note was gone, all right. Then she crossed to her own bed and pried the cupboard open. Carefully, she lifted the panel out, standing back in case rats came rushing out.

The food was still there, or at least some of it was. The plastic bags had been chewed to shreds, and the top of the cardboard box was littered with tiny black shards. Mice. They weren't as bad as rats, but now the food was ruined.

She closed the panel quickly and pushed it tightly into place. So, no one had found the cupboard.

Good. If the police figured out that she and Carlie had been stealing food, they might not bother to look for her.

Sarah slid off her bed. The room looked huge in its neatness, and she stood in the middle to consider the damage done to their special place. The room now looked and smelled like *her*, and Sarah suddenly hated it.

In an angry whirl, she yanked the covers back on her bed and pushed her robe off onto the floor, knocking over the doll dishes. Where were their pictures? She'd better not have thrown them away. In a fit of anger, Sarah jumped as high as she could and landed noisily on both feet. She jumped again and again. *Thud! Thud!*

Down below, her mother moaned.

"Sarah, settle down!" came her father's voice.

Sarah didn't answer. Let them come running up here, she thought. *I hate them. I hate her.*

Out of breath, she plopped down on her bed. She wished she could talk to Jesse, but the room was so neat there was not even any garbage to be taken out. The gas station would be locked up by now anyway.

Sarah knew it wasn't going to do any good for the police to talk to Jesse or the neighbors, either. They didn't even know the neighbors very well. Her mother always said people didn't want to be bothered. Besides, they weren't "her kind," whatever that meant. So there was Lew at the gas station—well, sort of. Sarah had never actually spoken to him. And Jesse. And Josephine—except they hadn't seen her for a long time. And the girls Carlie sometimes rode the bus with, but Sarah didn't know any of their names.

After Sarah got into bed, she pulled out her tablet. In the comforting darkness, she folded a sheet of paper into squares. In each square she drew a picture of a place where Carlie might have gone. A church—there was the Manito Methodist Church a few blocks from the school. They had bathrooms and a kitchen and might even have some food.

The library—it was warm there and, with the books, there would be plenty to do. Carlie could curl up and sleep in one of the stuffed chairs. Sarah drew the front of the library with a bike parked outside.

She took a deep breath and let it out again in shaky little rasps. Then she lay down on her pillow and followed her thoughts into Carlie's head, where the pictures were very clear. She was sitting on the bicycle seat and listening to her mother say, "Let her go. How far does she think she'll get?" She pushed off from the curb and rode away. Sarah could feel the hurting in her own heart.

In her mind, Carlie turned at the next corner and started to cry, feeling awful because her mother didn't like her and she was never going to wear a pretty dress for Jesse. She rode around for a long time until it was late—too late to go home without getting into big trouble.

Sarah's heart beat faster and faster as she rode along inside Carlie's mind. It was easy after all the years of being in this room together. But then she came to a curb, stopped and put out her foot to balance the bike. After that, the pictures went away.

They picked up again later. Now Carlie was walking, and it was cold and dark. Sarah couldn't imagine where the bike had been left or why. She knew Carlie had to find a place to get warm. Where would she go?

Maybe Carlie did try Josephine's, she thought, but knocked on the door and found no one home. Where would she go next? Most places, like a church or library, would notice a girl hanging around too long by herself.

But sometime in the middle of the night, staring through the bare tree outside the window, another picture came to her. It came in a flash, just like the answer in a nice, tidy math problem. With her heart bumping under her nightgown, Sarah squeezed her eyes shut. Sometimes the most obvious answer was the right one after all.

sixteen

SARAH WAITED FOR morning to come, staring at the ceiling as the darkness thinned to gray.

From her bed, she pushed aside the curtain and looked out. A layer of white frost covered the roof. Even the naked maple tree looked stiff with cold.

She pulled back the covers and sat on the edge of her bed with her feet curled inward, avoiding the cold linoleum. If Carlie hadn't gone where she imagined . . . She would be there; she just had to be.

Sarah got dressed quickly, sidestepping the places in the floor where she knew the boards would creak. She hadn't heard Dad get up for work yet, and she guessed they were both sleeping late after all that had happened last night.

Sarah crept down the stairs, placing her feet on the edges closest to the wall where the steps were most solid. The door at the bottom squeaked only a little as she turned the knob with her fingertips. She hesitated on the last step in case they had heard her, but no one stirred. Carlie belonged to her, not to them, and she wanted to be the one to find her.

Not daring to use the bathroom, Sarah carefully let herself out the back door, turning the lock slowly, taking care not to let it click. Over the years, she had gotten very good at sneaking, even better than Carlie.

She lifted her jacket off the hook on the porch, put it on and headed out. The early morning air stung in her nostrils, and she hurried across the crunchy, frozen ground toward the garage. Her blue bike seemed almost to be waiting for her, ready to go on this secret mission.

Sarah pushed it out of the garage and wheeled to the far side of the gas station, where she slipped into the women's restroom. A picture of Kim, walking sleepily into her own pale green bathroom, drifted across her mind. Sarah flushed the toilet, plugging her ears as if she could stop the sound. Jesse would be sure to hear the noise, but she'd be gone before he could get his shoes on.

On her bike again, Sarah carefully avoided the front of the station and finally headed down Sherman. Only the sounds of her own breathing and the whirring of her bike tires on the pavement kept her company as she leaned forward, pushing hard on the pedals. With each shove, her shoulder reminded her why Carlie had left in the first place, nearly three days ago now.

By the time she reached the house behind the old fence, her fingers ached with cold. Sarah parked her bike and pushed her hands into the front of her coat to warm them, then scanned Josephine's porch and her door and windows. The house looked closed up and empty, just as she expected, but Josephine's garage was the place she had come to investigate. It had occurred to her last night that Carlie would never break into a house, but she might hole up in someone's garage, if she knew the person who owned it.

As Sarah approached, she checked the house next door for a face at a window. Not seeing anyone, she went boldly to the little door on the side of the garage facing Josephine's house. Like the door in the Nevilles' kitchen, the top half was a window, and she cupped her hands to peer in through the grimy glass. Skittering along the ledge inside, a spider made its way to the edge and dropped out of sight. Deeper in the garage Sarah could make out the shapes of fenders, a car door with a shiny handle and several old tires—the car parts Josephine had told them about. Sarah knocked on the glass and listened. Nothing stirred. She turned the doorknob and pushed, only to find boxes stacked against the door.

She returned to the front of the garage, banged the big double doors and yanked on the padlock. Then she peered through the crack between the doors. The smell of mold and decay seeped through from the other side, but Sarah knew that wouldn't stop Carlie if she were desperate enough.

"Carlie?" she called out in a low whisper. "Carlie?"

Sarah watched her breath disappear in front of her. "Carlie. Carlie." When no one responded, she went back to the side of the garage once more. Her feet ached inside her shoes from the cold, and if she were already cold, Carlie must be freezing. She could even be sick.

Then something bumped inside the garage. A shifting box, or a squirrel, or maybe a person.

"Carlie!" Sarah shouted. If Carlie would just show herself, they could be out of here in ten seconds. She rose up on her toes to get a better look inside.

Sarah waited and listened again, a strange feeling creeping up her neck. It was as if someone were crouching just inside the door, holding their breath.

"Come on, Carlie, I know you're in there," Sarah called. "Carlie, Carlie, it's me, Sarah." She jiggled the doorknob and turned back toward the street. What now? She was making a lot of noise; any minute someone was going to notice her. Then her eye caught a flash of movement in the garage door window. Someone must have peeked out at her.

Sarah knocked again, harder this time. "Carlie!" She hammered on the door. "Carlie, open up!"

At last, boxes scraped the floor and the

doorknob turned. The door opened a crack. Sarah held her breath and cocked her head to see into the crack. "Carlie?" She felt her mouth open in the cold morning air.

"Quick," Carlie said, her voice low and trembly.

A swallow dropped down Sarah's throat as Carlie opened the door wider and grabbed her sleeve.

"Get in here," she said. "Someone could be watching."

Sarah slid inside the dim space and reached for her sister. "Carlie!" she cried. The girl she embraced felt cold and shaky. Even her hair, long and stringy, seemed cold. She looked damaged somehow, too, like a pretty plate with a chipped rim.

"I was afraid you might be dead! I didn't know." Sarah was suddenly furious. "The police found your bike!" she yelled at her. "How could you stay gone so long? How could you do it?"

Carlie looked at her now, her eyes as wide as a raccoon's that had been caught in the beam of a headlight. "I didn't mean to. I wasn't really going to run away, not at first." Carlie's chin quivered.

"This place is awful. It's freezing."

"I know." Carlie's shoulders pulled inward as if she were trying to crawl inside herself for warmth. "I slept over there." She pointed to a shadowy corner where Josephine kept a lawn mower, some shovels and a pile of gunnysacks. Carlie's hairbrush lay on the floor next to the pillowcase she had packed three days ago.

"What did you eat?"

"Just some shriveled-up potatoes." Carlie pointed. "They were terrible."

Below the window on the floor was a piece of moldy potato with white tendrils reaching for the light. Sarah shuddered.

"I didn't know what else to do. Josephine's back door is unlocked, but I was afraid someone would see me and call the police. I've been watching for her. . . . If she didn't get home by tonight, I was going to sneak in and get some food anyway." Carlie covered her face and started to cry.

"It's okay now," Sarah said. "You can come on home."

"No!" Carlie shouted it. "I can't go home. Not after what I did. She'll kill me. You know she will."

"We have to think of something," Sarah said. "You can't stay here."

Carlie scooped her hair aside with her hand. Her face was dirty and streaked from crying. She looked much younger than fifteen.

"I know," Carlie said. "I was thinking about waiting till Josephine gets back—she's got to come back pretty soon. Maybe I can borrow some money from her. Then I could go someplace. Oh . . ." Carlie's face dropped into her hands again, and her shoulders bumped with her sobbing. Sarah watched her, wondering what to do.

Always so stubborn, Carlie had never broken down and cried like this. Sarah didn't know how to make her stop.

"It'll be okay," she said. "You'll see. She's been upset that you're gone, and Dad's really been worried."

"I have to think," Carlie said, holding on to the sides of her head. "Maybe Jesse and I could go somewhere. If we could get Lew's truck . . ."

"No," Sarah said. "That would be stealing. And Jesse could already be in trouble. She cleaned our room; the police have your note."

Carlie gasped. "That note was *mine*!" Then her face grew serious. "Everything's gone wrong. I thought I could just stay at that house Jesse told me about for a few days. I figured they'd find a family for me to live with. I thought you could come, too, after awhile."

"You did?"

"Well, yes."

Carlie looked right into Sarah's eyes when she said it, and Sarah knew she meant *of course*, of course she would want her sister with her. Sarah swallowed past the lump in her throat. "Tell me what happened to you."

"I never even got to the home. Some boys knocked me off my bike and took it. I hit my head on the curb and I was dizzy." Fresh sobs racked

Carlie's shoulders.

"But the police are looking for you," Sarah said. "If you don't show up, they're going to think Jesse did something to you."

"No, I'll write a note, tell them she's going to beat me again."

"They won't believe you," Sarah said. "She's acting all weepy, like this is the worst thing that ever happened to her. One of the policemen was nice, but the other one thinks you're a troublemaker."

Carlie moaned as she rocked back and forth with her arms wrapped around herself.

"Wait, I know what," Sarah said. "I'll use Josephine's telephone to call Jesse at the gas station. He'll help us figure out what to do."

"I don't know. If he's in trouble because of me, he's really going to be sore." Carlie wiped at her cheek. "I don't want him to see me like this."

"It'll be okay. He'll help us."

"I don't know," Carlie repeated, rubbing her forehead.

"Come on, we'll go inside Josephine's house together. We'll be in there only a minute. Nobody'll see us."

Carlie nodded shakily, and the two left the garage and hurried into the house, where it was only a little warmer, and found the telephone sitting on top of a phone book in the kitchen. Sarah's fingers were so cold, she could hardly turn the pages, but she circled the number and managed to dial.

On the other end, the phone rang and rang until a breathless Lew answered. "Yeah, Phillips!" he barked.

"Is Jesse there?"

"Who's callin'?"

He sounded angry. "It's really important. Please."

Jesse must have been standing nearby, because the next voice Sarah heard was his.

"I found her, Jesse, but there's sort of a problem."

Carlie sat on a kitchen chair with her coat pulled tightly together at the collar, watching Sarah's face.

"Hey, the police hauled me downtown this morning. Tell her she's got to get back in a hurry."

"I was thinking maybe you could come down here to Josephine's. We need to figure something out. She's . . . sick," Sarah added. It was only a small lie. Carlie did look sick, and for all Sarah knew, she really was. In the light of Josephine's kitchen, her eyes looked as if they had sunk into her head.

Jesse seemed to have covered the phone and was talking to Lew. "Okay," he said. "I got a break comin' up. How do I get there?"

Sarah gave him directions. "We'll be out in the garage." She hung up and turned to Carlie. "Jesse's going to help us. He'll be here in a minute."

The girls hurried back out to the garage, and a

few minutes later, Lew's truck rattled into the driveway. An angry-looking Jesse got out and slammed
the door.

"He's going to be so glad to see you." Sarah
forced a smile for Carlie's sake, Carlie who was now
standing with her back pressed against a pegboard
wall, as if it were their mother who was about to
confront them.

Sarah opened the small door and stood back for
Jesse to enter. At the sight of Carlie, his expression
seemed to soften and his arms flopped to his sides in
a helpless gesture. "You little dunce," he scolded
her. "You can't just run off with no place to go."

Carlie looked frightened at first. Then her arms
went out and she cried, "Oh, Jesse," rushing to
where he was standing at the door. Her arms locked
around his waist and she fell against him, sobbing
again.

"It's okay. It's okay," Jesse soothed, patting her
back.

It was the most romantic thing Sarah had ever
seen, and, forgetting for a moment all the horror of
what was really going on, her heart fluttered at the
sight of Jesse holding Carlie and stroking her hair.

"Hey, hey," Jesse went on.

"I'm so sorry, Jesse. I didn't think . . . you'd get
. . . into trouble." Carlie cried so hard it sounded
like she would choke on her tears.

Sarah worked a linty wad of tissue out of her

jacket pocket and handed it to Carlie. "Here," she offered. "We have to figure out what to do."

Carlie moved away from Jesse and blew her nose. "Okay, fine, as long as it doesn't mean I have to go back."

"You do have to go back," Jesse said. He sat down close to her on some boxes and leaned forward on his elbows. "You know, you could be in trouble for breaking in."

"Into a garage?"

"That's right, and once you make a mistake, nothing works in your favor."

Carlie blew her nose again.

"Look, somebody's going to have to call the police," Jesse said. He stood up and pushed his hands into his pockets. "If we do it now, at least you can tell your side of the story. But we don't want them coming here. How about I take you back to the station; maybe they'll meet us there?"

Carlie was quiet while she seemed to think it over. "What will Lew say?"

"Don't worry about Lew. He's the greatest; he's been in worse fixes than ours. That's why he lets me stay there."

Sarah smiled while Carlie stared blankly at the floor. "She's going to get me for this."

"She's going to get you anyway," Jesse pointed out. "It may as well be for something real."

Sarah thought about his words for a moment.

Maybe Jesse understood their mother better than they themselves did.

Carlie sighed and moved slowly toward the door. "Well, I'm going on sixteen. In a couple of years I can get a job and go wherever I want and never come back again."

Jesse draped his arm around her shoulder. "Good girl," he said.

That was all. Carlie packed her few belongings back into the pillowcase, and they left the garage, carefully closing the door behind them.

Then Sarah got her bike and walked with it behind Carlie and Jesse to the truck. Earlier this morning she had expected to feel relieved, but now she could not quite hold on to that feeling. Seeing Carlie and Jesse together, something bigger now ached deep inside the secret places of her heart. Where would she ever find a place for herself?

seventeen

AT THE GAS STATION, the three made their way past a car on a hoist and a scarred wooden work-bench cluttered with tools, car batteries and odd parts. On the wall behind the bench was a picture of a rosy-cheeked woman in pigtails drinking Coca-Cola, smiling as if she didn't have a single problem.

"You can stay in here till they come." Jesse pushed the door open on his tiny room, no bigger than a closet.

"What's goin' on?" Lew came up behind Jesse and peered over his shoulder. With dark eyes and coarse mustache, he looked more gruff up close than he had from a distance.

"It's the girls from across the alley," Jesse told him. "There's a little problem, but we're getting it cleared up." He pulled the door shut, closing the girls inside his small room. Male voices faded into the gas station.

Carlie rummaged around for food and found two

216

dry-looking fig bars, which she devoured in just a few bites. She swigged them down with some orange Nehi from a half-empty bottle.

Sarah shuddered at the sight. Even their cupboard was better than this. She hoped they wouldn't be in here long. Jesse's room smelled like dirty laundry and gasoline. There were no windows, just a small metal lamp casting a light on the truck seat that was his bed. Draped over the seat were several blankets, and Sarah placed herself carefully on the edge to wait.

This might be better than living in an alley, she thought, but why should someone as nice as Jesse have to be here in the first place? And if Lew was so great, why didn't he take Jesse home with him?

Carlie set the empty Nehi bottle on the floor and burped. She sat quietly for a moment, then said, "I don't want to go back there. She's going to wait till Dad's gone and then . . . I don't know. I just don't know."

Someone rapped lightly at the door and Sarah opened it.

"They're here." It was Jesse. "Hey, don't let on about my room, okay? It's only temporary anyway."

"We won't tell," Sarah assured him.

Carlie stood up, pushed her hands nervously down the legs of her pants and let out her breath.

"Everything's going to be okay this time," Sarah said, knowing it wasn't true.

They followed Jesse through the station.

A man in a car at the gas pumps gaped at them as they approached the police car. Standing there were the same two policemen, Grimes and Thomas. Carlie sucked in her breath as if all she saw were the uniforms and guns and polished sticks.

"Carlisle Neville?" Grimes flipped open his notebook.

"It's Carlie."

"Okay, Carlie." He introduced himself and Officer Thomas.

"I ran away," Carlie said weakly.

"We know," Thomas answered with a little smile. "You're in a bit of trouble, aren't you?"

Carlie nodded.

"We'll need to know the whole story," Grimes said.

Carlie closed her eyes and let out a huge sigh. Then in just a few sentences she explained what had happened.

Grimes shifted his weight. "You mean someone got a spanking?"

"No-o." Carlie's face flushed.

"Look," Jesse jumped in, gesturing toward the Nevilles' house. "I'm telling you they're getting knocked around over there. "

"You've seen something, then?" Thomas said. "Do you recall any dates?"

"Well, not exactly, but I know."

Sarah could tell Grimes still didn't believe them.

Lew, who had been watching from the gas pumps, sauntered over to where they were all standing. "Look, officers," he said in a calm voice, "how about giving the kids a break, huh? I've had this station for years. That woman who lives over there is plum nuts, if you ask me."

Plum nuts? What had Lew seen? Sarah wondered. Had he heard Carlie screaming?

"That's interesting," Grimes said, and he beckoned to Thomas. They walked away a few feet and talked in low voices.

"Thanks," Sarah said. "We're telling the truth."

"I know," Lew said, patting her arm. He turned back to the station, where another car had pulled up.

When the policemen returned, Grimes said, "Okay, here's the deal: We don't know what happened or didn't happen. We'll take you home and have a talk with your folks."

"I don't know," Carlie said. "We're already in trouble." Sarah knew she was thinking that telling the police had been a very bad idea.

"But you have to do *something*," Jesse said. A third car pulled in. The station was busy today. "I guess I'll have to talk to you later, okay?"

Carlie whispered, "Okay," and he hurried back to the gas pumps.

Then the girls were ushered into the back of the police car, where they sat on wide leather seats. Sarah was grateful that they wouldn't have to walk across the alley and go in through the back porch with two policemen following.

Riding the short distance around the corner to the front of the house, Sarah ceased to see anything in their future except a deep, dark hole. She took hold of Carlie's hand on the seat between them. Her sister's fingers felt bony and cold as they squeezed her back.

"Okay, girls," Grimes said as he stopped in front of their gray house. "Come on, let's see what we're dealing with." Everyone got out. The car doors slammed.

Dad was the first to appear at the front door, hesitating in the doorway, then coming out onto the walk. "Margaret, it's Carlie!" Sarah thought he blinked back tears, but she wasn't sure. He took several steps to meet them, then squeezed Carlie's shoulders and let go again quickly. "Where in the world have you been? Are you all right? Why didn't you call?"

"I've been at Josephine's by myself," Carlie told him. She didn't say anything about the garage. "I know I should have called. . . ."

Their mother, still dressed in her robe, hung back. She stood rubbing her arms as if to stay warm in the open doorway. Sarah looked away.

"Thank you, thank you," Dad said, reaching out to shake the two officers' hands. He took a deep breath and let it out again. "I was beginning to. . . well, we're so glad to have her back."

"Can we go inside?" Officer Thomas said. "We'd

like to talk to all of you."

"Oh. . . yeah, sure," Dad said, looking surprised.

Carlie hooked her limp hair behind her ear and walked beside Sarah up the steps. Their mother avoided both of them, looking straight at Grimes.

"So," she said, "she was fine all along. I'm sorry; you must have better ways to spend your time."

"No, ma'am, this is our job," Grimes said.

Everyone stood uneasily in the living room. Sarah tried to breathe rhythmically as if her breathing were the only thing that would keep her from getting sick. *Don't tell on your mother*—it wasn't just her rule; it was a rule set down by the universe long before Sarah and Carlie had been born. Everyone knew it.

Sarah took up a place next to Carlie in front of the piano. Their mother arranged herself on the edge of the couch with Dad standing at her side. It was almost as if they were all gathered to hear how much the bill was going to be. Their mother would write out a check for finding Carlie, and that would be the end of it.

Officer Thomas flipped his notebook closed. "Well, we've had a chance to talk to Carlie and her sister."

Their mother's cold gaze flew across the room at the girls and back again. "Oh? What did they tell you?"

Sarah waited. Dad shifted and pushed a hand into his pocket.

"The specifics aren't really important," Thomas

said. "The thing is, Mrs. Neville, whatever is going on in this house isn't working, and it could be—"

"Well!"

Sarah stole a glance at Carlie. Here it came.

Their mother drew back against the couch as if she were trying to be absorbed into it. "I . . . it's obvious you're blaming *me* for this." She stared straight at the girls.

"No, ma'am," Grimes put in quickly. He hitched his gear more closely around his middle. "What you hafta do is talk to your kids before things go this far."

"Talk! I've tried to talk to them, but they just clam up, both of them. All I ever hear is 'I don't know,' or 'nothin'.'"

"Well, I know what you mean, ma'am. It could be that taking Carlisle out of the situation for a while would be a good idea. Maybe we can find her a home out in the country for a few months. Be good for the girl. Good for everyone."

For both of them?

"Certainly not!" their mother answered. "This has been bad enough without enduring that kind of humiliation. The whole town would know. I can just imagine!"

"It's a new program we're trying out," Grimes went on.

"We just got her back," Dad said. "Surely, you can understand."

Carlie continued to stare into space without saying

222

a word. Sarah could not tell what she was thinking this time. She had said she didn't want to go home, that for a while she had hoped a foster family would take her. But what if they couldn't go together?

Their mother lit a cigarette and blew smoke up into the room. "You can't take her." She cocked her head and sniffed. "Not after all this."

While Thomas talked about cooperation and family, their mother puffed hard on her cigarette. He finished with, "Maybe your church minister could help you work things out. This seems like a nice enough family."

Dad, who'd almost never been inside a church, said, "I don't think we're going to need a *minister*."

The two policemen looked at each other. Even Sarah could tell they were trying to help.

"Well, I'll tell you what we're gonna do this time," Grimes said. "We're gonna let this go for a while. Keep an eye on things. If we don't hear from you folks again, well, that would be good."

Sarah could almost see the air in her father's lungs come rushing back out. "You have our word," Dad said. "You won't be hearing from us again."

It was the right answer. Grimes nodded, snapped his notebook shut and moved toward the front door with Officer Thomas.

Dad followed. "Watch your step on the porch." He mumbled a friendly goodbye, then closed the door and bolted it.

Immediately, the house fell into an unnerving stillness, with their mother in a trance on the couch. Sarah could not think of one word to say, nor did she want to be the one to speak. It was as if the walls themselves were holding their breath. Instead, she retreated from the living room without waiting for permission. Carlie did the same. Through the kitchen and up the stairs, they moved with their usual stealth into the safety of their private domain.

Without commenting on the unnatural neatness, Carlie went straight to her bed and climbed onto the middle, pulling the quilt up around her. Sarah sat down on her own bed. They did not go to the grate. Whatever happened next would be loud enough for them to hear from any corner of their attic bedroom. They stared straight across at each other while they waited.

From where Sarah sat, she could see the police car pull away from the front curb. She heard it slow, then turn onto Grand. We're on our own again, she thought, and struggled to fathom the size of the crime they had committed this time. Ten seconds later the girls heard their mother hoist herself up off the couch and storm through the kitchen. Dishes rattled in the cupboard as she passed.

"Margaret," Dad called after her.

The door at the bottom of the stairs banged as their mother yanked it open. It was the same sound they'd heard before, and Sarah knew what it meant.

eighteen

"HOLD ON, MARGARET," Dad said.

A scuffling sound followed. "Don't touch me!"

"We've got to talk."

"Well, that would be a first!" The two of them argued at the bottom of the stairs, then moved back into the living room, where they lowered their voices.

Sarah and Carlie slid carefully off their beds to the grate.

"Sit down," Dad said. "Just . . . sit down."

"I'm not going to have a *child* call the police on me," she wound up. "The very *idea!*"

Now Dad's head moved into view as he paced between the living room and the dining room. "I think the officer may have a point, Margaret."

Sarah leaned away as cigarette smoke drifted up through the vent. Carlie sat across from her looking pale and tired.

"*The officer may have a point!*" their mother

mimicked. "What would you know about it? The great floor polisher!"

"Yes, that's what I am."

His voice fell *plunk* at the end of his sentence. Usually, Dad didn't say much in an argument except "Uh-huh, uh-huh."

"I do the best I can," he added. Then his voice grew sharper. "Look, you've been miserable since we moved out here from Kentucky."

"That was nine years ago! What's that got to do with it?"

"I know, nine years is a long time. I thought you'd be happy here where your sister couldn't one-up you all the time; isn't that what you wanted? It was your idea to move, not mine."

An uncomfortable silence followed. Sarah heard the *foosh* of cushions as they sat down in their respective places.

"Well, I won't have two snotty girls holding me hostage. I just won't have it!"

Snotty girls. As always, the words stung. This didn't sound like it was going to blow over very soon.

"Couldn't you have defended me?" their mother railed on, "instead of just sitting there like a lump? How could you let them talk to me like that?"

The bickering went on and on. Every time their mother said something, Dad said something back. Each of his comments was clipped as if he wanted it to end the argument.

Finally, his chair creaked. His footsteps came through the house to the stairwell. The girls scrambled back to their beds.

"Carlie," he called in a soft voice. "Come on down here."

Carlie's eyes widened. "What's he want?" she whispered.

Sarah shrugged. She couldn't guess. It was usually her mother's job to call them downstairs. Carlie got up quietly and went down, while Sarah waited on her bed.

Their mother followed Dad into the kitchen. "I don't know why you're making such a fuss over her."

"For crying out loud, Margaret," Dad snarled back. "Your daughter probably hasn't eaten anything decent in *three days*. And she needs *a bath!*"

Silence again. Sarah had never before heard Dad talk like this to their mother.

"Go ahead, Carlie," Dad said. "Get in the tub. I'll fix you some breakfast."

"Tt! She's got you right where she wants you." Sarah pictured her mother folding her arms and sneering as Carlie passed on her way to the bathroom.

The water in the bathtub came on, sounding deliciously warm. If only Sarah could get into the tub, too—she hadn't had a bath in three days, either, but this was no time to ask. She waited, knowing Dad would fix enough breakfast for both of them.

By the time he finally called her downstairs, he had fixed oatmeal, bacon, juice and pancakes. He piled the pancakes and bacon on a platter and set it in the middle of the kitchen table.

Carlie sat down across from Sarah, her hair hanging wet and her face scrubbed pink.

"Margaret," Dad called, sounding calmer now, "I wish you'd join us."

"I'm tired," their mother said, and she passed through the kitchen to the bedroom. Her shoulders were curved toward her chest, and she looked almost sick. She stopped for a moment in the bathroom as if she were checking which towel Carlie had used. Sarah cast her eyes down, focusing on her plate.

When they were finished eating, Dad announced he was going to work.

"But Carlie just got back," Sarah argued. "Do you have to leave?"

"I have so much catching up to do," he said. "We've got to keep a roof over our heads. You girls see if you can get a nap." Before he went out the back door, he took Carlie in one arm and Sarah in the other and hugged them against his plaid shirt. Sarah squirmed with embarrassment. If her father had ever hugged her like this before, the memory of it was gone. He left, the back door closed, and they were alone in the house with their mother.

Sarah peeked through the bathroom at a rosebud robe and white legs stretched out on the bed. The bedroom door on the other side blocked her mother's face, so she couldn't have seen the hug. Good, Sarah thought. If she were angry about the breakfast, she'd be furious about the hug. But Sarah could tell by the limp look of her legs that she was already asleep. Maybe she *had* been worried. Maybe she hadn't slept very much last night, either.

Sarah herself was beginning to feel weary now that she'd eaten so much breakfast, and she followed Carlie back upstairs. Her shoes fell with a thump to the floor, but she didn't care about the noise. All she cared about was that Carlie would still be here when she woke up from this nap.

Carlie fluffed her pillow and pulled her wet hair up over her head, then lay down carefully, as if the feeling of her own bed under her was something new and wonderful. She let out a long sigh. "Nothing worked right," she told the ceiling.

"Jesse was worried," Sarah said, lying back on her bed. "He took me to look for you downtown."

"He did? I think he really likes me."

Sarah's heart bumped. How nice it would be to have someone else who cared about her. "I sort of have a boyfriend, too," she announced.

"You do? Who?"

"His name's David Henley. I met him at the library."

"Gee," Carlie said, "a lot has happened since I left . . . and I missed it all." She squeezed her eyes shut in a pained look. "I've caused so much trouble . . ."

She told Sarah how she had wandered around, trying to figure out what to do, and had finally ended up at Josephine's house.

"I never even thought about coming home," she said. "I didn't think she'd let me in, anyway."

"I left your quilt outside for you," Sarah said.

"I wouldn't have thought of that, either, but thanks."

"I'm glad you're home," Sarah told her. "You're not mad at me, are you?"

Carlie rolled toward her, hugging her pillow. "No, I guess not." She looked around the room.

"Our pictures are gone."

Carlie frowned, but she didn't really seem to care. "I just want to go to sleep and dream about something nice. I don't even want to think about what's going to happen to us now."

"It'll be okay," Sarah said. "We'll stick together."

"I should have waited for you that day. None of this would have happened if there had been two of us out there."

Sarah felt her throat tighten. Things might not have turned out any better if Carlie had waited, but hearing her say so was worth everything.

"Does your shoulder still hurt?" Carlie asked.

"Not much. I wondered if it was broken, but it's getting better now." Sarah's eyelids drooped. There was a lot more to talk about, but it would have to wait. Overwhelmed by the comfort of the bed, she pulled the edge of the quilt over her and finally went to sleep.

When Sarah woke many hours later, the sun was beginning to set. She felt groggy and unreal. Carlie stirred and looked over at her, then jerked her head toward the window.

"Oh, no!" Carlie exclaimed. "We slept all day long."

Sarah got up and pushed the curtains open. A pink and blue sky filled in the spaces behind the bare limbs of the maple tree. She listened for sounds in the house. Her father would still be at work; maybe he would even stay late to catch up. She crept over to the chimney and peered down into the room below. Only a pale light from the living room windows illuminated the waffle pattern of the grate.

"She's still asleep," Sarah said.

"I wish she didn't have to wake up at all," Carlie remarked. Some of her old energy seemed to be back. "I wonder if she'll ever speak to us again."

"She has to speak to us sooner or later."

"I suppose she'll make me apologize about the dress."

"No," Sarah said certainly. "You can't apologize. You should have seen how it was at Kim's house; everything was different. Her parents let her go everywhere in the house, and she even makes popcorn in the kitchen. You can't apologize. Not now."

Carlie hesitated. "She might kick me out for good."

"I'd go with you."

"Well, I won't go in her room ever again. Not even if she begs me. Not even if the rest of the house is on fire."

Sarah laughed.

A short time later, a ping hit the bedroom window. Carlie jumped up and flung the windows open.

"Hi, Jesse. Everything's okay, sort of. I'll come out to the garbage cans later if I can."

Jesse said something else and Carlie giggled. Then Jesse laughed, sounding light and happy. Sarah crept to the window where she could peer out at Jesse.

"Shh! You'll wake her up." Carlie waved, then closed the window carefully and went back to her bed, where she sat with her hands folded neatly in her lap.

"I think I love Jesse," she said. Her face had that glow, the same one she'd had the night she read Jesse's note. "I never thought Dad would call the police."

"We were real upset," Sarah said, sitting down next to her sister. She would never tell how her mother had dressed up for the police and cooked a

232

special dinner. "Carlie, what was it like in Kentucky before she got like this?"

"Just normal," Carlie said. "Aunt Janey came over once with roller skates for my birthday. She and Uncle George were rich, I remember that much, and they had this huge shiny car."

"Was I at the party, too?" Sarah asked.

"You were in the stroller. They brought you something, too, a little turtle. It made me mad, I remember, because it was my birthday."

"I don't even remember Aunt Janey."

"She was pretty," Carlie said, "and had the most beautiful clothes" She laughed. "Dad says I'm getting to look just like her, but I wouldn't know about that."

Sarah stared out at the bare maple tree and thought about this. Did her mother secretly want to go back to Kentucky, to live in the big old house again? Maybe she'd had her own bathroom there, a bathroom she didn't have to share with anyone.

"I wonder how long she's going to sleep." Sarah got up and crept toward the stairwell. "Maybe I'll sneak downstairs and go to the bathroom."

"She probably wouldn't do anything to you," Carlie said, "not after Dad yelled at her."

"I'll be real quiet." In the semi-darkness, Sarah crept slowly down the stairs. The kitchen looked gray and unfriendly. No lights shone in the house anywhere. Only the sounds of her own breathing went with her past the sink and into the bathroom.

She scooted carefully across the floor in her stocking feet, past the tub to the second door. Against the light from the bedroom window, she could see her mother's legs still lying relaxed on the bed, exactly the way they had been that morning. Carefully, she pulled the door toward her, but did not let it click. Then she opened the toilet lid and sat down, feeling a warm relief, praying she could finish before she heard the sudden sound of bedsprings.

Too bad they didn't have an upstairs bathroom. If they did, they wouldn't even have to see their mother. She could just leave plates of food on the bottom step once a day, like in a prison. The thought made Sarah snicker, and she put her hand to her mouth to stifle the sound.

She flushed the toilet, plugging her ears. She'd be in worse trouble for not flushing than she would for waking her up, but the water filling the tank was so noisy. When it was finished, Sarah took her fingers away from her ears and stood perfectly still. Not a sound came from her mother's bedroom.

She reached for the doorknob and gave a little shove. The door swung wide open. Her mother lay on the bed with her face pointing straight up. Sarah could just barely see the outline of her nose against the bedroom window. She watched for a minute, until the thought occurred to her: her mother was not moving at all. She did not even seem to be breathing.

nineteen

SARAH RUSHED BACK through the bathroom and up the stairs. No voice rang out to yell at her for being noisy.

"You made it," Carlie said, congratulating her. "Maybe I'll go down, too."

Sarah caught her breath. "No, you can't. There's something wrong. She didn't even roll over when I flushed the toilet."

"Really?" Carlie bent over in the center of the room and flopped her hair over her head, then began brushing it toward the floor. "We'll probably hear her coughing in the kitchen any minute. There won't be any dinner tonight, you can bet." Her voice sounded upside down, too, as she continued brushing. Finally, she stood up, tossing her long hair back so it settled around her shoulders. The old Carlie.

"Maybe we should check," Sarah said. "Or do something."

"Like what?"

"I don't know." Sarah rushed to the grate, where she could peer down into the living room below. After a minute, Carlie joined her. They waited and listened for sounds, but there were none.

Finally, the telephone rang, slicing through the silence.

"I'll bet that's Kim," Sarah said. "She told me she'd call."

The girls raised their heads and waited while the phone rang and rang. They did not go downstairs to answer it. But their mother didn't get up to answer it, either.

Now Carlie seemed alarmed, too. "I wonder what's going on. Did you see her face or anything?"

"Not really," Sarah said, "She's lying there just like she was this morning."

"Geez," Carlie said. She went to the head of the stairs and looked down, balancing herself between the railing and the window ledge. "She was so furious."

"I know," Sarah said. "Now she hates him, too—all of us."

Carlie turned a pale face toward Sarah. "I wonder if she . . . you know, did something to herself."

Sarah's scalp crawled at the thought. "How could she have? I mean, she went through the kitchen and straight to bed."

"Oh, brother," Carlie said. "Whatever this is, it's going to be my fault. I just know it."

"No, wait. Maybe she's pretending, just to get

back at us. But she wouldn't do that. Would she?" Unable to come up with an answer, Sarah moved close to her sister. Horrific pictures ran together in her head—bloody wrists and empty pill bottles.

Then anger replaced the pictures. *You'd better not have done anything! Just who do you think is going down there to look, huh?* In her mind, Sarah sounded just like her mother, and she felt ashamed of her ugly thoughts.

"Maybe she got sick or something," Sarah concluded. "She can't get any madder if we go check."

Carlie nodded. "Okay. If she wakes up all of a sudden, we'll tell her we were worried."

For the third time that day, Sarah crept carefully down the stairs. She felt Carlie breathing behind her as they descended, hesitating to listen every couple of steps. Sarah remembered going through a haunted house one time. It had felt just like this—not knowing what would jump out from behind the curtain.

At the bottom of the stairs, Sarah and Carlie stood together in the semi-dark kitchen, peering through the bathroom to the bedroom on the other side.

"See," Sarah whispered.

The streetlight out front illuminated their mother's silhouette on the bed as if she were a corpse laid out for a wake. Together, they advanced into the bathroom, then again stood watching, waiting for some movement.

This didn't make sense. Sarah hesitated with her hand on the light switch, afraid to flip it on. She feared that her mother would suddenly come to life—and that she wouldn't. Finally, unable to bear the suspense any longer, she turned on the light. Both she and Carlie jerked back.

Their mother lay stretched out with her arms at her sides and her eyes fixed on the ceiling.

Was she alive, or not? Sarah peered closer, her hand to her mouth.

Suddenly, the eyes rolled toward them, and Carlie clutched Sarah's arm.

"Go away. Leave me alone." The sound came from deep within their mother's throat as if she were disconnected from the words. With a heave, she tried to raise herself onto her elbows, but failing this, she flopped back down. At the same time she began to shiver—little shivers at first, and then her legs began to bounce up and down.

Sarah and Carlie watched without moving, as if what they saw was too intensely interesting to be interrupted.

Within a few seconds, their mother was trembling so hard her bones seemed almost to rattle. Her hands clutched at her body as if she were trying to hold herself still. Her head turned toward them on the pillow, her eyes round now as if she were shocked to find herself shaking like this.

Carlie let go of Sarah and stepped forward. "Mama?"

Mama! Sarah shot a look at Carlie. Whatever was happening must be enormous—they hadn't used that word in a long, long time.

"What's wrong? Tell us," Sarah begged. She held onto the doorjamb, being careful not to step into the forbidden room.

"This sh-sh-sh-ak-ing," their mother stuttered. "I . . . c-c-c-can't stop."

Carlie covered her mouth, and Sarah wondered if she was going to throw up. Grabbing her sister's elbow, she pulled it to her. Both girls stood in the doorway, staring dumbly, while their mother continued to quiver on the bed.

"We have to do something," Sarah said.

She waited a moment for Carlie to move, but when she didn't, she whirled away, turning on lights in the kitchen and dining room as she made her way to the telephone. She didn't know her father's number by heart, but she knew how to look it up now. Flopping open the book, she read Nelder, Nemeyer, Neville Floor Care. Sarah circled it with a pencil and dialed, praying someone was there to answer. "This is Sarah Neville. Could I talk to my dad?" The words tumbled out sounding surprisingly light.

In just a second, he was on the other end of the line. Lucky. "Is anything wrong?" he asked right away.

Sarah's voice shook as she tried to explain.

When she returned to the bedroom, Carlie was still standing in the doorway. Their mother now lay with her arms wrapped around herself. The quivering subsided, then started up again.

"Do you need a blanket?" Sarah asked.

Their mother nodded weakly, and the girls bumped into each other getting to the knitted blanket at the foot of the bed. They unfolded it together and let it float into position over her. They didn't touch her. They didn't sit by her on the bed. They didn't tuck in the blanket. It seemed like the only thing to do was back out of the bedroom and watch from the doorway.

"Dad's coming," Sarah offered. "He'll be here any minute." Then they waited.

It seemed to take him hours to get home, though the little clock on the nightstand said it was only a few minutes before Dad's truck showered the walk with gravel from the driveway. He rushed in the back door and past the girls. They moved out of the bathroom to wait in the kitchen.

"Can you stand up, Margaret?" they heard him ask. "Here, let me help you."

"I c-c-can't get up," their mother said.

"Is it your legs? Are you cold?"

When their mother started to sob, Dad hurried into the living room, ignoring the girls, and dialed the phone. "This is Hal Neville." He gave the address. "There's something wrong with my wife. She's been real . . . nervous." He described what was happening. Then he said, "Yes. Okay. How long?"

"An ambulance is on the way," he told Sarah and Carlie on his way back through the kitchen. "Margaret, it's okay. We're going to take you to the hospital."

"Oh, brother," Carlie said, and Sarah could almost hear her swallow.

No one in their family had ever gone to the hospital in an ambulance. Several years ago, Sarah had stood in the street and watched a woman being carried out of her house on a stretcher. But the woman had been old, so it had seemed okay. Now Sarah listened for a siren, but there was none. Instead, the front doorbell rang after a while and she went to answer it. Two men in plain blue shirts stood there. They didn't have a stretcher or anything, but a white ambulance sat at the curb.

Sarah led them into the bedroom.

"Mrs. Neville," one of the men said, "did you take anything? Pills or anything?"

"N-n-n-o. Just . . . make me stop sh-sh-shaking."

A few minutes later, the men came out with their mother walking jerkily between them. They each held her by one elbow. Dad followed behind, stuffing her rosebud robe into a brocade bag.

The girls stared as she passed by them. Tears streamed down their mother's face as she struggled to stay upright. She looked at the girls with an expression Sarah could not decipher. She seemed embarrassed, angry and afraid all at the same time. Maybe she didn't want them to laugh at her. Or maybe she was trying to say she couldn't be their mother anymore.

"I'll be home as soon as I can," Dad said, and they left through the front door.

Sarah and Carlie watched as the ambulance lights disappeared down the street. Dad followed in his truck. When they were out of sight, the girls stood in the middle of the kitchen and looked at each other without speaking.

Sarah couldn't put a name to her own feelings. Her stomach felt like it held a whole jar full of moths, but at the same time she knew something momentous had just happened. Something had exploded, and the pieces were flying off into outer space.

twenty

IT WAS NEARLY midnight before Dad came home. Sarah and Carlie had said everything they could think to say upstairs in their room. Feeling too guilty to watch television or listen to the radio, they had finally gone downstairs to make sandwiches, and Carlie had taken a long time with the garbage. From their places at the table, they looked toward the back door as Dad shuffled into the kitchen, his face pale.

Seeing him like this, Sarah's heart lurched. "What happened?" she asked.

"Well," Dad said, dropping his keys onto the windowsill. "Your mother . . . she's been unhappy." He seemed to be struggling for simple words. "The doctor's a little worried. He says she'll have to stay in the hospital for a while."

"Oh," Carlie said with a sideways look at Sarah.

"She's going to be fine, though, just fine."

Sarah pushed the salt shaker around on the table. *Just tell us; we aren't little girls anymore, you know.*

"Will she be home in time for Thanksgiving?" Next week.

"Well, no, not that soon, but Christmas for sure. I'm going to see if Josephine will consider coming back for a while."

Josephine? Sarah looked from her father to Carlie and back again. She wanted to smile, but that didn't seem right, not when their mother was in the hospital.

The next night after school, the girls came home to Josephine. A woman on the radio was singing about love, and Josephine sang along like she always did as she folded the towels.

When she saw the girls, she hugged them both against her soft chest. "Your dad won't be home for dinner," she said, releasing them. "He's stopping by the hospital to sit with your mama. How've you two been? Not too good, I'm hearing."

"I stayed in your garage for a couple of days," Carlie told her. "Did he tell you that?"

"I heard," Josephine said. "If I'd known you were coming, I would have cleaned the place up." She laughed. "Anyway, you don't have to explain anything. But, your mother, is she going to be okay?"

"Dad says she's going to be fine," Sarah said.

"Good. Now, what's on your agenda today?"

At last Sarah smiled. It was so good to have Josephine back.

Carlie took off for the gas station, and Sarah

244

called Kim. They were on Chapter 11 of *Amalthean Summer*.

"Kim, do you want to be on my *agenda*? Ask your mom if you can come over today." Sarah had decided she had a few weeks to invite Kim over, a short time to be just normal in this house. After that, who could tell what would happen?

Sarah held the phone away from her while Kim squealed. Then she hung up and dashed around the house, picking things up and straightening pillows on the couch. In her room, she pushed socks and papers under the bed, dancing from one thing to the next.

Half an hour later, Sarah watched Kim get out of her mom's car and come flying up the front walk in a bright red coat.

Sarah hurried to the front door with a sense of pride. The house had never seemed so open, so free. This was where she lived, and now she had a visitor who was here just for her.

Sarah swung open the door with a flourish. There stood Kim with that huge smile on her face, and Sarah smiled back. Today there was nothing to worry about. No one would come in the back door to catch them doing something they weren't supposed to do.

Kim stepped into the living room. "I couldn't wait to get here," she said. "Now I can find your house on my bike whenever we want." She glanced around the room, dropping her book on the couch.

Sarah skipped ahead through the kitchen, pausing

to introduce Kim to Josephine, then led her friend up the narrow stairs. This was the moment Sarah had dreaded. It was as if the room upstairs was part of her, and if Kim didn't like it, she couldn't like the person of Sarah, either.

All the way up, Kim stretched her neck and finally peered up over the railing. "Oh!" she said when the chimney came into view. "I wish I had a secret room like this. You're so lucky. My mom and dad walk right past my door all the time." She seemed in awe of the slanted ceiling and the paned windows that opened out onto the roof. "This is so wonderful," she said. She sat down on Carlie's bed and gave a little bounce.

Sarah felt her lips pull toward her ears in a grin. She knew how silly she must look, but she just couldn't stop smiling.

They ate cookies in the living room, Kim straddling the piano bench and Sarah on the couch.

"I just love your house," Kim said. "It's so . . . interesting."

Interesting. Sarah liked that. Could it be that having an old house with a chimney in the bedroom was something special? There was just one more part to the test, and that was introducing Kim to Carlie. Would Kim, after all, see Carlie as just another runaway? Would Carlie think of Kim as a child?

Sarah fell into an awkward silence, listening for the back door to open. But when Carlie finally entered the kitchen, then the living room, Kim looked up and smiled.

Quickly, Sarah spilled out the words. "Kim, I'd like you to meet my sister. Carlie, this is Kim."

"Hi," Kim said. She didn't look nervous at all. Then all three of them sat in the living room and talked about high school. Sarah didn't have to do a thing. Her two best friends seemed to like each other.

On Thanksgiving Day, the girls stayed downstairs in the kitchen to help with the dinner.

Sarah leaned close to Carlie and whispered, "Why don't we see if Jesse can come?"

Carlie looked shocked. "Oh, I couldn't. I'd never even be able to swallow with him here in this house, in front of Dad."

"Why not?"

"Just *because*."

Sarah guessed there was more to love than she understood, and she let the subject drop. Still, she hated to think of Jesse alone in that room with nothing but Nehi and fig bars.

While the turkey roasted, she and Carlie made salads together, stuffed celery with cream cheese, and emptied cans of cranberries into a glass dish. Sarah watched her father's face. What could she say to him? Most other days he'd been at the hospital, and they hadn't been alone with him. What kinds of things did Kim say to her father?

Dad mashed the potatoes, humming while he worked. When he was finished, he lifted the beaters without turning them off and shot white blobs around the kitchen. Some of them stuck on the ceiling.

Sarah and Carlie looked up in time to see several of the blobs fall off onto the floor.

Dad, who had not laughed in Sarah's recent memory, now tipped his head back and let forth with a deep roar. Soon all three of them were laughing, a sound that seemed out of place in this kitchen.

Then as suddenly as it started, Dad stopped laughing and dinner was served in the dining room. Sarah had carefully skirted her mother's chair at the head of the table and set the special china on three other sides.

Sarah mounded her plate with mashed potatoes, turkey, dressing, cranberry sauce, candied yams, stuffed celery and a roll. She drizzled gravy over all of it and started to eat. The only sounds in the room were of silverware touching the china and a few satisfied murmurs.

After they had eaten, Dad wiped his mouth and placed his cloth napkin next to his plate. "I really miss your mother," he said, staring at the table.

Sarah stopped chewing and exchanged looks with Carlie.

"You miss her, too, don't you?" Dad asked.

How could they answer this? Josephine was back.

Kim had been here. The girls had taken long baths, alone. They hadn't even thought about stashing food upstairs. Now their mother was going to be home before Christmas.

"Uh-huh," Sarah said, because she knew it was expected. Something was missing in the house all right, but that something was hard to describe. There was no point in listening at the grate anymore. There was no need to whisper at night, and they hadn't played Draw-in-the-Dark in a long time.

Sarah remembered how Officer Grimes had said families needed to talk. That might be true, but how could they talk about *this*? Even though no one had said the words out loud, she knew what they were. Their mother had *gone crazy*.

Dad was talking, something about her making good progress at the hospital. "She loves you, you know."

Sarah took in a deep breath. She felt words forming behind her lips that wanted to come out. She wished Carlie would be the one to talk, but she was beginning to see that Carlie couldn't. Something had happened to her when she ran away, something inside her mind. It was as if the stubbornness was gone, and now she was just sad. Sarah didn't like it, feeling like she was the one who needed to be fifteen.

But this was their only chance to talk to Dad, these days while their mother was away. And even if it made him angry, maybe Sarah would have to tell him how things had been. "She doesn't even like us," Sarah heard herself say, "She wishes she'd never had any kids."

Dad glanced at Sarah, then at Carlie. "Where did you get an idea like that?"

Come on, Carlie, say something.

Carlie looked pained.

"It's true," Sarah went on. "She doesn't want us around. She won't let us come downstairs. We can't go in the bathroom or get anything to eat."

Dad looked puzzled, as if he'd never noticed any of this before. "Well," he said after a long pause. "Your mother can be difficult." His voice dropped off as if that were the end of the discussion.

Sarah slumped with a sigh and wiggled her shoulder in defiance. This was more than being *difficult*. This was *mean*. Anger against her father grew in her chest as she looked at her sister. She and Carlie communicated without even saying anything. A set of the mouth or a narrowing of the eyes. Carlie always got the message. But her father needed words, and even then he didn't seem to understand.

"We're scared of her," Sarah persisted. "Kim isn't afraid of her mother."

Carlie smoothed her napkin while she stared at their father's face. Sarah waited for her to say something, but her mouth was set.

Dad shook his head. "For heaven's sake, there's nothing to be afraid of. It's not like she's been beating you!" he said. "It's just that she's young. She wasn't ready for two girls." He forced a smile. "You know, your mother was only seventeen when I married her. I was in the Air Corps." He rubbed his forehead as if he could wipe away any unpleasant thoughts. "Her parents didn't want us to get married, but I just had to have her."

Sarah shot a look at Carlie, who raised her eyebrows. *I just had to have her.* Maybe he'd been happy because he got the girl he wanted, but their mother had been miserable after a while. Not quite able to grasp the thought that was trying to form, Sarah tried again. "We're not afraid of Josephine. She likes us."

Dad said nothing. He just gazed at the wall in the dining room as if a picture of their mother were hanging there.

Why didn't he ever look at *them*? Sarah wondered. Was there something wrong with them after all? But no, the problems had started when they were too little to know any better, so how could it have been their fault?

Sarah fixed her gaze on Carlie, telling her in their secret way that this might be their only chance to talk to their father.

Carlie shifted her weight and folded her arms protectively across her chest. "Sometimes she does beat us," she began. "It's true."

twenty~one

CARLIE TOLD HIM about the dirty towel and the bathrobe strap. "She choked me . . . I couldn't breathe." Carlie's voice quivered, but at least she'd said it.

Dad sat with his elbows on the table and his hands clasped under his chin, with no thoughts registering on his face at all. Abruptly, he stood up and began clearing the table.

"Well," he said, "she must have been . . . I don't know." He stacked one plate on top of another, knocking a fork onto the floor.

Sarah picked it up and looked into his gray eyes as she handed it to him. His expression reminded her of someone watching a movie, as if the story was interesting but had nothing to do with him.

The girls followed him into the kitchen with dishes of leftover food.

Sarah covered the cranberry sauce and put it in the refrigerator, leaving the door open longer than she had to. Her chest ached with an uneasiness as she stared at the blur of food and brightly colored containers. Their father had reduced their story to nothing in one sentence, but Sarah knew she couldn't let go of this now that it had started.

She closed the door and turned to her father. "Look." She pulled down the collar of her shirt. After all this time, the skin on her shoulder had settled into a yellowish scar.

"How'd you do that?" Dad asked.

"I didn't do it." Sarah stared at him, willing him to hear what she was saying.

He turned to Carlie as if he sensed a conspiracy between the two of them. Then the puzzled look on his face slipped slowly into understanding, his face reddened and his cheek twitched. "Your mother did this?" he asked.

Sarah nodded.

"Why?"

Carlie spoke up again. "She was trying to hit me with one of her wooden hangers, except Sarah got in the way." She hesitated. "I tried on her black dress. I know I shouldn't have. . . ."

"Hmm." He reached for Sarah's shoulder. She flinched.

"I'm not going to hurt you." He looked surprised for a minute, then ran a big finger along the scar. "It's not broken, is it?"

"No," Sarah answered. "It doesn't hurt that much any more. It's just a little stiff."

"She must have been pretty angry. I can't imagine . . ."

Sarah waited for him to say something more, but he didn't. "Does she have to come home next week?" Sarah asked boldly.

Carlie nodded. "I don't think she wants to be here."

Dad sat down heavily at the kitchen table. "That's not true. Your mother loves all of us, she really does." He paused and played with his hands, locking and unlocking his fingers in front of him. "I was going to tell you tonight after dinner. Dr. Pederson thinks it would be a good idea if she went to Kentucky for a while. She and Aunt Janey have some patching up to do. So you're right, I guess she's just not ready to be home with us."

Sarah felt a wave of relief, but she wondered why they couldn't have a mother like Kim's, one who had pictures of them on the wall? Someone who would sew them dresses. Why couldn't they come downstairs without permission? There were no reasons, it was just the way it had always been.

Dad's eyes were getting misty. "But you have to understand, I love your mother more than anything. She was so beautiful when I met her. I figured she'd do something special—be a musician, or a dancer." Then he gave a little laugh. "I never did know what she saw in an old guy like me. Something, I guess."

There were a lot of things Sarah didn't get, and this was one of them. She did not believe she could love someone who would hurt her children, and she was positive that someday she'd know that for sure.

"She hopes you'll come to the hospital this weekend," Dad told them. "If all goes well, she'll be discharged on Monday or Tuesday, and I'll pack her a suitcase and take her straight to the train station."

So she won't have to come here.

"Janey will be good for her," Dad added. "Don't worry, we'll work this out; we always have."

No, we haven't, Sarah thought.

After dinner, Dad headed back to the hospital. The girls made up a turkey dinner for Jesse and folded waxed paper over the top. They weren't really leftovers, Carlie said, because they hadn't been in the refrigerator yet.

Together, they walked to the gas station and rapped on the front window until Jesse appeared. He seemed embarrassed when he opened the door. "Oh, hi," he said. "Um...come in." He laughed nervously and led them back to his room. "At least we can sit down in here."

The three of them lined up on the truck seat while Jesse gulped down the food. "I miss this," he said. "My mom could really do turkeys. I'd almost like to go home, but . . ."

"But what?" Carlie asked, her voice sounding soft.

"Nah, it'd never work out. My dad, well, my *stepdad*, we never got along. Some things just don't work out."

"We don't know if things are ever going to be okay in our family, either," Sarah told him.

When Jesse had finished eating, the three of them

headed back across the alley. Sarah ran a little ahead so Carlie and Jesse could hold hands. She didn't mind anymore. Maybe someday Jesse would be her brother, a thought that made her heart flutter. If he married Carlie, he would be their friend forever, and he would have someone to love him.

Sarah said good-bye and went into the house. Carlie came in just behind her, looking bright and happy. Later, in their room in her nightgown, Sarah confessed, "I don't want to go to the hospital."

Carlie nodded in agreement.

"You know what I figured out about Dad?" Sarah asked.

"Yes. You figured out that he knew."

"Yes," Sarah said. "He had to know what was going on. He just didn't want her to get mad or leave him; that's all he ever worried about."

"I know," Carlie said solemnly. "She acted like she was something special, and he believed her."

Two days later, they climbed into Dad's truck. Sarah sat on the bump in the middle with her legs sprawled onto Carlie's side. "What should we say to her?"

"Well, just tell her you love her," Dad said, but Sarah knew she wouldn't be able to do that.

"She's been doing a lot of talking with her doctor. There are things you don't know about her growing up in Kentucky."

"Like what?" Sarah asked. In her mind she saw the perfect house and all the oak trees, eighteen of them. She saw the two princesses who lived there.

"Well, your grandfather was a bull of a man and made life pretty rough sometimes. Her life wasn't so perfect, not like she makes it sound. She has to think about all that."

He stopped at a light, shifted down and waited for the green. "I guess some of this is my fault for not paying attention," he admitted. "I should have . . . oh, I don't know. I should have done something. But running a business is hard work. I always thought if I could just make more money . . ."

He didn't look at them, just stared out at the traffic lights hanging above the intersection and went on. "I still think the job is a good idea. It's not dancing or music, but your mother is a pretty good businesswoman. Since she came to work in the shop, things have picked up a little. We might even be able to afford a decent Christmas for a change." He patted Sarah's knee, startling her. "In fact, with your mother coming back on the twenty-third, I'd say it's going to be a wonderful Christmas."

For someone who didn't talk much, Dad seemed to have a lot to say. The light turned, and they went another few blocks to the hospital. Sarah wished it were farther away, so she could get her thinking straight. But maybe she never would.

They parked and went into the hospital, past a row of wheelchairs and into the elevator. The operator, a woman in a gray uniform, asked them which floor and cranked the lever. Sarah busied herself looking at a sign attached to the wall. POLIO VACCINE: PROTECT YOUR CHILDREN NOW!

The elevator stopped at the fifth floor, and Dad led them down the hall to the right. Sarah looked nervously into the rooms they passed. What would she see? she wondered. People with wild hair chained to their beds? No one seemed to be in their rooms.

Their mother was not in her room, either, but her flowered robe was draped across a chair. It seemed strange to see it there, a place not their house. A nurse in a white, pointed cap showed them down the hall to the activity center.

Sarah pulled in her breath, but her lungs would not fill. She wanted to hold Carlie's hand, or feel her father's arm across her shoulders. Her heart pounded harder and harder with each step until she thought it would explode. Somewhere a radio played a lively tune, out of place in these white halls.

"Here we are," Dad said. They slowed down and peeked into a large, brown room with bubble gum--colored furniture. About twenty people, all dressed in regular clothes with combed hair, sat in wooden chairs at tables around the room. They all looked up.

One woman sitting just inside the door had found a piece to a jigsaw puzzle and was tapping it into place. Several others worked on Christmas decorations made out of felt and sequins. A couple of men played checkers. Sarah felt embarrassed for them, doing such childlike things. She hadn't expected this.

"There she is," Carlie whispered, "over there."

Sarah looked. Their mother was sitting far to the right at a tall, black piano, dressed in her red shirt and corduroy pants. She wasn't playing the piano, but her left hand rested on the keys and the other turned pages of the sheet music in front of her. Dad broke away and strode toward her. When he touched the back of her neck, she turned around and let him kiss her cheek.

Then she looked over at Carlie and Sarah. Her face was as pale as a white onion. Sarah's first thought was that she needed time to watch, to decide what to think. But her mother was looking at them, almost smiling, then pulling it back. Her arms opened as if she wanted her daughters to rush to her.

Sarah's feet seemed glued to the floor. She couldn't move even if she had wanted to. Carlie's arm pressed hard against hers, and their fingers touched for just a second. Carlie must be thinking the same thing: What was the trick? When would the words come flying at them?

When neither girl moved, their mother's smile slipped away completely and she looked questioningly up at Dad. *What's going on?* she seemed to ask. Then with an impatient sweep of his arm, Dad motioned to them to join them.

I can't, Sarah thought, but her sister moved forward and she followed. In a moment, they were both bending stiffly and hugging their mother, giving her little pats on the back and straightening again quickly. Sarah had never noticed before that she had such bony shoulders.

"What's the matter?" their mother asked. "I'm well scrubbed."

Sarah forced a smile. The worst was over.

The visit went on for an hour with Carlie and Sarah sitting on wooden chairs, listening mostly to talk about the way things worked at the hospital.

"How's it going at home?" their mother asked them finally.

"Oh, fine," Carlie said.

"That's good."

"We've been keeping the kitchen real clean," Sarah added.

"Good, good," their mother said.

"The girls have really been pitching in," Dad told her.

"I knew they would."

When it was time to leave, they all hugged again, their mother sitting at the piano while Sarah and Carlie bent to reach her. Even here at the hospital, her clothes smelled faintly of violets.

On the way out the door, Sarah turned back and saw her mother with her hands braced on her knees, watching them leave. Her expression was blank, as if she didn't know what thoughts were in her own head.

"It's not going to be easy," Dad said on the way home, "but we're going to have to make it work. We're stuck with one another."

Stuck. It was the only word Sarah heard.

twenty-two

THEIR FATHER HAD not stopped smiling all morning. "This time tomorrow your mom will be home," he said again. He stood at the kitchen table and counted out dollar bills into two neat piles.

What's that for? Sarah wondered. Money had always been invisible in this house, the bills paid somewhere out of sight. When he was finished, he handed one pile to Sarah and another to Carlie. "Here, I want you girls to go downtown and do some Christmas shopping—buy your mother something special."

Dad grinned proudly as Sarah fingered the wrinkled green bills. He'd given them more than twenty dollars apiece. He must have waxed a hundred floors.

"Can we get something for you, too?" Sarah asked. "And each other?" Last year they had made watercolor paintings for gifts. Now her mind went wild with thoughts of the wonderful things she could buy.

"That's the idea," Dad said. "She'll like that—lots of presents under the tree when she walks in."

The night before, they had put up a tree in the living room, turning its flat side toward the wall. Dad let them hang the ornaments wherever they wanted while he watched. It didn't look as perfect as when their mother decorated, but with mugs of hot chocolate, and Perry Como's Christmas program on television, it had been fun.

Their mother's train schedule had been tacked to the kitchen wall since she left home three weeks ago, and Sarah had subtracted the days in her mind: *Twenty days. Fifteen days. Five days. Don't get too happy now, it's all over on the twenty-third.*

But today Sarah refused to worry—today they were going Christmas shopping with a pocketful of money. She didn't even care that it was raining an icy drizzle. Suddenly, Sarah felt festive.

She dressed up in a blue jumper, a white blouse, white anklets and her good shoes. She and Carlie stood in the bathroom and shared the mirror while they brushed their hair.

When they were finished, Carlie stepped back and looked at herself in her green dress. "Do you think my waist looks smaller?" she asked, cinching in her belt.

"Maybe," Sarah said. Her waist looked the same as always, but lately Carlie had been measuring and remeasuring every few days. Before their mother left, she had not seemed interested in that kind of thing.

They walked to the corner of Thirty-eighth and Grand just in time and climbed on a crowded bus that smelled of wet wool in overheated air.

"Here's two," Sarah said, swinging into a seat. Carlie sat down next to her and settled in. Sarah looked around at the other people. Some of the women wore hats and gloves. A little boy was wearing a bow tie and knitted mittens. In spite of being dressed up, though, most of the people looked straight ahead without expression, as if going downtown were the most ordinary thing in the world.

Sarah could hardly sit still watching the blocks move past. She patted her pocket several times, checking her fold of money.

By the time they reached Riverside, the rain had turned thick and white. People hurried along with their coat collars pulled up. The girls stepped off the bus and moved straight to the enormous windows of The Crescent department store, where a crowd had gathered.

"Oh," Sarah gasped. Cotton snowflakes floated down on the heads of dolls that skated around tracks on blue mirrors. In the next window, real-life children were lined up to see Santa Claus, who was seated on a throne made of candy canes. Sarah and Carlie stood watching until their feet got too cold to stand any longer.

In the doorway of The Crescent, a man in a blue

coat and trim cap stood ringing a bell. The sound of a trumpet playing "Hark, the Herald Angels Sing" blared out from the next block.

Sarah wondered if she would see the alley kids and their puppy. She hoped not. She hoped they had all gone home or found someplace to stay by now.

She counted the bills in her pocket for the third time. "Dad says we should get her a special present," she said.

"Maybe something about music," Carlie suggested. She pushed open the big glass doors, stenciled with a gold letter C. The girls stepped inside onto polished wood floors.

Everywhere they looked, green, red and white wreaths with silvery tinsel decorated columns or walls. In the middle of the store, a big gold cube of a clock hung from the ceiling. The ornate black hands pointed out 2:10—they had the whole afternoon to shop and to be part of the crowd hurrying through the aisles.

"Let's go to the second floor; that's where the good stuff is," Carlie suggested. Next to a wide flight of stairs, an elevator whirred behind ornate metal doors.

"Two, please," Sarah said to the operator.

The woman sat on a little stool at the lever and pulled it. *Whoo-oosh. Clunk.* "Second floor, watch your step." The doors opened to more decorated columns and little round tables draped to the floor with red and green felt.

"Look, over here," Sarah said, pulling Carlie to one of the tables. "These are about music." She picked up a ceramic carousel horse and wound it up. The tune that tinkled out sounded delicate and sad.

Carlie picked up another and wound it up, too. Soon several different tunes played at once as the horses moved up and down on their bases.

"How about this one?" Sarah said. She picked up a beautiful black horse wearing a white saddle and a wreath of lavender flowers around its neck. It seemed to be a match for their mother's violet perfume and bath salts.

"Oh, yes," Carlie said, "this is the one. How much?"

Sarah checked. "We could go together on it. Five each," she said.

They paid for the horse and smiled at each other as the saleslady wrapped it in tissue and laid it gently in a green box with gold lettering on top. "This is really special," Sarah said, and Carlie nodded.

They pooled their money for Dad, too, on a shirt with soft brown elbow patches, then stood in the aisle planning how they would split up to buy each other's gifts. Sarah waited for Carlie to disappear between the shelves, then headed out of the store.

It was snowing now, wet splats that turned to slush as soon as they hit the walk. Sarah hurried across the street to the big, cluttered Woolworth's store. Inside, colors seemed to jump out at her in happy confusion, the shelves stocked with all kinds of interesting and inexpensive things. She picked up a shopping basket and began filling it with items she knew Carlie would love: red nail polish, a new hairbrush, a gold hair clip, a little mirror on a stand, a ring with a green stone and the December issue of *Seventeen*.

On her way to the counter, she stopped at a shelf of diaries with tiny locks. Sarah chose one with a kitten on the front for Kim—only seventy-nine cents; she was sure Dad wouldn't mind. Adding the numbers in her head, she calculated that she still had enough money for bus fare and a Coke with Carlie.

When they met again under the clock at The Crescent, Carlie was carrying a small box and a bag with The Crescent logo. She seemed very pleased with herself, smiling and rolling the top of the bag so nothing showed.

The girls went up the elevator to the luncheonette on the top floor and sat a long time at a table next to the wall. They shared a piece of warm cherry pie and sipped their Cokes slowly.

Sarah could hardly wait now for Christmas, though in the corner of her mind there persisted that feeling of dread. As hard as she tried to think only happy thoughts, the worry crept back in among the presents and their shopping trip. Everything could be spoiled as soon as their mother got home. They could be shut away again in their room, wondering what they would eat.

By the time they finally left the store, snow fell steadily between the tall buildings. Sarah stopped by the bell ringer and dropped the rest of her money into the kettle, except for her bus fare home.

Carlie put her money in, too. She held up the small box she'd been carrying. "I bought this for Jesse. It's a little electric pot that can do soup and popcorn and everything. All he has to do is plug it in."

Sarah smiled, feeling a rush of warmth for Jesse. "I wonder what he's going to do on Christmas."

"I don't know. We'll find a way to take him some dinner, for sure. At least he's got a place to sleep."

Shoppers rushed by as if they were trying to out-run the weather. Sarah and Carlie went to wait at the bus stop, snow settling on their hair and coats. It was sticking now, and Riverside was striped with wide black tire tracks.

The girls sat without talking on the bus as it ground its way to their neighborhood. Sarah studied her reflection in the darkened window and went over every detail of their day, in case they didn't get to go shopping like this again. Tomorrow, their mother would be downstairs under the grate again, watching television and smoking.

Back home, Sarah wrapped her presents behind the chimney while Carlie wrapped hers on the floor between the beds. Sarah wondered about their father watching television downstairs alone. Was he worried about tomorrow? Or was he just excited, believing things would work out?

When the girls were finished, they trooped down the stairs with their stacks of brightly colored packages.

"Here comes Santa Claus," Sarah sang, and Carlie joined in. Colored points of light glinted off the shiny glass ornaments, bringing the living room to life.

Dad looked up as the girls passed him on their way to the Christmas tree. He smiled. "What do we have here?" he asked.

"Presents," Sarah said as if he couldn't tell. Amid the scent of pine, she and Carlie knelt by the tree and arranged the gifts among several others that had arrived in the mail. Carlie's present for her was wrapped in an oblong box with a red bow and a candy cane attached to the top. Sarah squeezed the box, wondering at the squishy feel. She looked questioningly at Carlie, but Carlie just grinned.

The next day, Dad whistled and jingled the coins in his pocket until it was time to warm up the truck. "I guess I'll be going," he said, "in case her train gets in a little early."

"We could put out a plate of cookies," Sarah offered.

"That'd be good," Dad answered. "Well, I'd better hurry now. The traffic could be heavy, too. You never know." He went out through the back door, leaving the girls to wait by themselves. He had not invited them to go along, and that was okay with Sarah.

Snow lay in a white blanket on the world outside. All morning a kind of wary excitement had hung in the air—the snow, Christmas, and now their mother coming home.

"She's been gone a long time," Carlie said as she spooned out cookie dough onto a baking sheet. "She could be different now." She sounded more optimistic than usual.

"Or she could be just the same," Sarah countered. This time she was the negative one. She took one sheet of gooey cookies out of the oven and slid the next one in.

After the last batch came out, the girls stacked the cookies on a platter—three dozen minus the four they had already eaten—and placed it in the center of the kitchen table where their mother would be sure to notice them. Sarah had been watching the clock all morning, and it was now just an hour before Dad's truck would pull in again.

While they waited, Sarah and Carlie sat on the floor near the tree and rearranged the gifts, shaking them and fluffing the bows. They tried to guess what was in each box. The hour crawled by, but finally, they heard the sound of tires on the snow-covered driveway.

Sarah jerked toward the sound. She had thought she was ready, but now her heart felt like it had dropped in an elevator.

The girls scrambled to their feet and ran through the dining room to the window. Their mother was just getting out of the truck, looking strange after all this time, with her hair brushed away from her face. She wore a beige coat Sarah had never seen before, probably Aunt Janey's.

"Should we go upstairs?" Sarah asked.

"No," Carlie said. "We aren't going to do that anymore."

"Okay, we'll stay here. It'll be our new agenda."

Dad reached into the back of the truck for the suitcases. The girls watched their mother come up the walk, stop to wait for Dad, and then gaze up at the house as if she had forgotten what it looked like.

Out of habit, Sarah shrank away from the window, but she was too late. Their mother saw them and smiled, a brittle little smile that Sarah could not interpret. Then she moved on, Dad right behind her, and a moment later the back screen door opened.

Sarah swallowed.

"Here goes," said Carlie.

From the dining room, they heard the sound of feet stomping off snow and the rattle of the back door. Their mother did not speak as they entered. Sarah imagined her looking around the kitchen for anything out of place.

"Anybody home?" Dad called in a cheerful tone.

Sarah and Carlie took up positions next to the dining room table where they could see into the kitchen.

There she was, looking larger than normal in her beige coat. As she brushed her hair back with her fingers, her eyes went to the cookies. "Who made those?"

"The girls," Dad told her.

"Oh, that's nice." Her presence filled the house suddenly, as if someone had turned on the television too loud. Coming into the dining room, her gray eyes locked with Sarah's.

In that one instant, the house seemed to shut down again and the walls moved in to enclose Sarah so tightly that she couldn't breathe.

At the same time, their mother's face brightened. She stopped, looked at each of the girls and then reached out her arms toward both of them. "Dr. Pederson says I have to *forge a new relationship*."

Dad beamed while the girls stepped closer to hug her, one on each side. The coat felt cold, but underneath she seemed a little less bony than when she was in the hospital.

Their mother stood back from them and said, "I'm going to try to do better. I really am. But you're going to have to help me."

Dad nodded behind her as if he were trying to send instructions to the girls.

"Okay," Sarah agreed, not sure what she was saying. Didn't they always try?

"For one thing," their mother plunged on, "I've quit smoking. Everything all at once. I'm going to be a little crabby, the doctor said." She laughed. "So, what else is new, huh?"

Sarah stared at her. Her mother's mouth straightened as if she could tell her joke wasn't funny.

"Quitting smoking," Sarah offered. "That's good."

They exchanged a few words about how things had been at home, then Carlie edged toward the kitchen. Sarah could hardly wait to get upstairs herself. Maybe they weren't going to hide anymore, but they couldn't undo years of feeling out of place in one day.

Their mother seemed to notice. "You can stay down here for a while, can't you? I see you put up a tree."

"Yes, stay downstairs," Dad urged them. Then he carried the suitcases into the bedroom.

Their mother took off her coat, dropped it on the couch and looked around the living room. "Maybe it's this house that's been the problem," she said after a minute. "It's so dark and gloomy."

It's not gloomy, Sarah thought. It's *interesting*.

The girls stayed in the living room throughout the afternoon and evening, sitting by the tree and leaning their backs against the couch. Their mother chattered like she did when she'd been dancing the night before. She described in detail how she and Janey had stayed up half the night talking and drinking tea, and how they had driven out to the country to see the twenty acres and the big house again. They had laughed about old boyfriends and teachers they had both had.

"The owners have put in tennis courts, but the trees, they're enormous, and, of course, the road out front is busy all the time now."

She said she was so glad she had gone and that she and Aunt Janey had decided they would visit at least once a year from now on. After a while, Dad got up and yawned. "I think I'll go to bed early," he said. "You must be tired, Margaret."

Their mother looked up at him and said, "Not just yet, Hal. I'm going upstairs to spend a little time with my girls. Dr. Pederson says . . ."

My girls?

Dad looked disappointed at first, then surprised, and finally pleased.

Sarah wanted to be pleased, too, but she wasn't. The idea of their mother being in their room for no reason felt like an invasion of their private place, like when she had gone up there to clean for the police. Her mind did a frantic scan of their bedroom: the beds, the floor, their closet, the window ledges. What had they left lying around this time that they didn't want her to find?

twenty-three

THEIR MOTHER FOLLOWED Sarah and Carlie to their room. "These stairs are so steep," she said as if she'd never climbed them before.

Moving past the chimney, she ducked down under the angled ceiling and sat on Carlie's bed. The girls claimed places on Sarah's bed, across from her. All three sat with their hands in their laps.

After a strained minute, their mother pulled up one knee and locked her fingers around her leg. "So," she began, "did you have a good time while I was gone?"

"I guess so," Sarah said. Was this a trick question? she wondered. Was she really asking, Did you miss me? "It was pretty strange," she added, just in case.

"I had a good time with Janey. I didn't think I would. We never got along all that well."

"I know," Carlie said.

"We weren't like you girls—you know, best

friends. In fact, we never even shared a room." She laughed nervously. "You don't share rooms in a big house like that."

Sarah offered a smile. "We like being in the same room."

Carlie nodded.

"I was always a little jealous of you two," their mother went on. "You had each other. You never needed to talk to me. I didn't have that with my sister. Dr. Pederson said it was as if she belonged to my mother and I belonged to Dad. Maybe he's right. Janey got all the pretty clothes and I got, well, rides on the tractor."

Sarah watched her face, her forehead wrinkled with emotion, and suddenly their mother looked like a little girl sitting there on Carlie's bed. A little girl riding around on a big ranch with no one to talk to.

But why would that make you treat your own kids the way she had? They hadn't been there, so what did a tractor have to do with them? Sarah looked around the room, at the squares of wallboard and the slanted ceiling and the chimney. They had lived up here for a long time. And every time their mother had come up the stairs in the past, they'd been terrified. Why hadn't she been up here just to talk to them, to tell them these things about her and Aunt Janey?

Carlie shifted next to Sarah as if she were trying to figure out what to say to this revelation. "But you had your piano lessons, and you were so good at it. Why did you quit?"

Sarah had always wondered the same thing.

"Oh, I was never that good at it," she answered. "Not like Janey. She was the one who had the talent. And then when she married George with all that money and they couldn't have kids . . ." She looked away from them. "I thought she still had all the advantages."

What was she trying to say? That she had been mean to them because Aunt Janey never had to put up with kids, and she was jealous? The more their mother talked, the less Sarah understood. She wished she would just say what she meant in a way that would answer her questions. *Do you love us? Are you sorry you had us? Why did you hit me like that?*

Talking was sometimes harder than it seemed. You couldn't just open your mouth and have the right words come out.

Sarah studied her mother's face. She herself had spoken up a few times lately, and that made her feel good. But asking the big questions on her mind . . . Did she dare?

"So," their mother said, "what do you think about all this?"

There was Sarah's opening, and she heard herself ask, "Do you love us?" Her face burned with embarrassment.

Carlie stiffened. Their mother looked shocked for an instant. Then she said, "Well, of course I do. What kind of a question is that?"

When Sarah didn't respond, she added, "I suppose I haven't always done right by you girls." Then she shook her head a little and straightened. "But you're just going to have to forgive me. I have my problems too, you know."

If they could only stop being *afraid* of her. Forgiving was something else. She hadn't said anything about the dress or the hanger or anything else that mattered to them. Were they supposed to tell her it was okay, that it was nothing, that living in this room and not being able to eat or use the bathroom was okay?

Sarah's mind flew back to the hanger. *My dress! You witch. Take it off!* The ugly words came slamming back to her. *You sneaky slut! Get out of my house!* She wished she could make the words and the way she had felt that night go away. But she knew that some of it would be with her for a long time, no matter what their mother said.

Yes, they knew she had her problems, too. But still . . .

"Dad never really told us what happened to you," Sarah ventured. "You're going to get well, aren't you?"

"Well, I guess I had a nervous breakdown. But it's more than that. My life . . ."

Her words trailed off, but Sarah watched her face. What she understood was that being unhappy could make you sick, sick enough to go to the hospital. If Carlie hadn't come home, might Sarah herself have ended up in the hospital with her legs shaking?

"Yes, I'm definitely going to get well," their mother went on. "I have to."

Their father opened the door at the bottom of the stairs. "Everything okay up there?"

"It's fine," their mother said. "I'll be down in a minute." Her mouth pulled into a flicker of a smile, but then it was gone. "Dr. Pederson says I should go back to my job. Or get another one." She stood up, letting out a little laugh, then took a deep breath as if she were glad this talk was over. Maybe she'd been planning what she'd say on her way back from Kentucky. It was clear she had promised her doctor.

As their mother turned to leave, she stopped by one of Sarah's pictures pinned to the wall. The tablet paper had been folded into four squares for drawing in the dark. Taking it off the wall, she looked puzzled. "Oh, this is . . ." She seemed to be searching for a compliment she could give Sarah to go along with her new, friendlier personality. "This is . . . I don't get it."

"It's just a game," Sarah said. "It's kind of hard to explain."

Christmas Eve seemed stiff, but more fun than any Sarah could remember. Earlier in the day, Kim and her mother had stopped by the house so the girls could exchange gifts. Sarah opened hers right away, a cute plastic dog with a flashlight nose.

Later, the family stood behind Mom at the piano and sang along while she played page after page of Christmas music. She wore a full-length gray and gold satin robe tied at the waist with an enormous red sash—a gift from Aunt Janey.

Sarah looked up at her father, amazed that he had such a deep singing voice. He rested his hand on their mother's shoulder and sang out in apparent bliss.

Afterward, the girls sat on dining room chairs turned toward the television while their parents sat in the living room in their usual places. They watched *The Adventures of Ozzie and Harriet*, *The Life of Riley* and *Our Miss Brooks*. Sarah was surprised to see that Miss Brooks was tall and blond; she sure didn't sound blond.

On Christmas morning, the sun came out. Christmas was not supposed to be sunny, but the day seemed perfect anyway. Sarah couldn't wait for everyone to open the presents she had bought. Their mother let the girls sit on the couch while she took the piano bench. Dad perched on the edge of his chair, ready to hand out gifts.

Their mother's eyes glistened with emotion when she opened the carousel horse. As she sniffed, she wound it up and played the tune over and over. "Where did you ever find this? I probably don't deserve such a nice present."

"Of course you do, Margaret," Dad said, kissing the top of her head. "Doesn't she?"

Sarah nodded.

Their mother had brought back gifts from Kentucky for each girl—identical boxes of note cards and new slippers. Aunt Janey had sent sets of cologne, soap and powder.

Dad handed Sarah's box to Carlie. "This looks interesting," he said, shaking it a little.

Carlie smiled and looked at Sarah in their private way.

"I hope you like it," Sarah said.

Carlie opened the box and began unwrapping the individual gifts. "Oh!" she exclaimed as each one was revealed. She looked at herself in the mirror and ran the brush through her hair. She put on the ring and flipped through the magazine. Then she opened the nail polish and pulled out the little brush.

"I don't know about red polish," their mother commented. "Isn't red for grown women?"

"Carlie's nearly sixteen," Dad said. "It's okay."

Carlie screwed the top back on and smiled a huge smile in her sister's direction. The gifts were perfect, Sarah could tell.

Next, Dad handed Sarah a present. It was Carlie's gift to her. She cradled the box on her lap as she removed the candy cane and tore the paper, cherishing whatever was inside already. It was from the person in the world who knew her best, would always know her best. Even if she got married someday and had a dozen kids.

Sarah peeked under the tissue paper. "Oh, Carlie!" She pulled out a pale blue nightgown with satin bows and little roses at the neck and sleeves. Sarah squashed it against her nose. It smelled as fresh and new as a whole department store. A nightgown of her own, new and clean and never worn by anyone.

"How nice," their mother said.

Sarah wrapped her arms around her sister's neck, and Carlie hugged her back for a long time. "Thank you, thank you, I can hardly wait to put it on."

At five o'clock the doorbell rang. By their mother's request, the girls were still downstairs sitting in front of the Christmas tree. She was in the kitchen working on their holiday dinner alone.

Dad answered the door, and there stood Jesse, holding a bouquet of red and white carnations with a plastic Santa on a stick in the middle.

"Hello, Mr. Neville," he said politely. "Is Carlie home?"

"Yes, yes, she's right here," Dad said, stepping aside.

Carlie jumped up as if she'd been caught in the act of doing something terrible. "Jesse!" Her face turned a deep pink. "Dad, this is Jesse. You know, he works at the gas station?"

"Oh, yes," Dad said, "the Phillips station."

Jesse stepped awkwardly into the living room. Somehow he'd gotten a bath. His hair was combed to the side, and his face was clean. He didn't look like Jesse at all, except for the grimy fingers that held the flowers.

Sarah stood up, too. "Hi, Jesse. Merry Christmas."

"Thanks, sister. I'm leaving for Lew's in a few minutes," he said. "We just closed the station." Jesse shrugged, then smiled. "Lew's wife is real nice, and all his kids are going to be there."

"Well, sit down for a minute," Dad said. "Would you like something to drink, some Coca-Cola maybe?"

"Sure."

Dad disappeared to get the Coke, and Jesse reached into the bouquet of flowers. He pulled out one red carnation. "For you, little sister." He handed it to Sarah, surprising her so thoroughly that she couldn't think of a single thing to say. At least he hadn't given her the Santa, as if she were a little kid. At that moment, he was the most handsome boy she'd ever seen in her life. More handsome than any movie star, more handsome than David Henley.

Jesse gave the rest of the flowers to Carlie, and when she hugged them to her, Sarah thought she looked exactly right, like a homecoming queen or a magazine model. Her dark hair hung around her shoulders, mingling with the flowers, and her face glowed a soft peach color. Their mother must have looked like that once, when Dad first met her.

Sarah wondered if she would ever be that pretty; she guessed maybe she would by the way she felt tonight. Carlie just had a head start on her.

"I have something for you, too," Carlie said, holding the flowers to her chest as she reached under the tree for the wrapped box.

"Gee, you didn't have to do that." Jesse's face was scarlet.

"You can open it at Lew's," Carlie said, handing it to him.

"I will. Thanks."

Their mother came to the doorway and looked in, familiar annoyance flashing across her face. Her eyes went straight to the flowers Carlie was holding.

"This is Jesse," Carlie stammered. "From the gas station. Across the alley."

Jesse nodded in their mother's direction.

Sarah felt a nervous stirring in her stomach.

"Oh." Their mother tensed for just a second. "Well . . . do you . . . are you going anyplace for Christmas dinner?"

"Yes, ma'am. I am."

"Oh, that's nice." Her face relaxed in an expression of relief.

It's okay, Sarah thought. At least their mother had asked, something that never would have happened before.

Dad returned with the Coke in a glass with ice cubes, and Jesse stayed another few minutes to drink it and talk. When he was finished, he said good-bye to everyone and set the glass on top of the piano.

The instant the door closed, Carlie and Sarah nearly collided as they lunged for the glass. Carlie got to it first and wiped away the wet ring with her sleeve. Their mother stared at them with her mouth open, but she went back into the kitchen without a word.

A little before nine, Sarah and Carlie finally returned to their room, each balancing a stack of gifts as they maneuvered up the narrow flight of stairs. Sarah changed into the blue nightgown and new slippers. She held Carlie's mirror away from her and looked at herself, then twirled around the room, pleased with the elegant way she felt.

There had been other Christmases when their mother had been happy; she liked Christmas. There had been presents then, too—not as many, but some. Yet the happiness had never lasted, and it wasn't going to last this time, either, Sarah knew that now.

"Nothing ever really blows over in this family,

you know," Carlie said, as if she were reading Sarah's mind. "She can't stay in that good mood forever."

"I know," Sarah said, "but I've decided to have a positive attitude. She might not be any different, but *we* are. We have friends now. Dad knows what happened to us."

"Maybe Jesse was right—you have to tell."

"It's like turning on a flashlight to see what's there," Sarah said, feeling very wise tonight. "Once you shine the light, you can't *un-shine* it."

Carlie tossed her pillow over next to the chimney. "Come on, they're watching TV. There'll be some good shows on tonight." She turned off the bedroom light and arranged herself against the bricks, tucking her legs neatly to the side of the grate.

"We could have stayed downstairs this time," Sarah said.

"I know, but I didn't want to, did you?"

"No, not after dinner was over." Sarah propped up her pillow. "I wanted to get up here to talk." Then over the sound of the television, she asked boldly, "Carlie, do you really love Jesse?" In the dim light from downstairs, she saw her sister grinning.

"Well," Carlie said with a soft sigh, "I love him today."

"So do I. I mean . . . I love him as a friend."

"Then you *like* him."

"Yes," Sarah agreed. "I like him a lot." By next Christmas, she would be thirteen, a teenager. Teenagers were old enough to be in love. Who would it be? she wondered.

Sarah felt her face flush. "Come on, let's play Draw-in-the-Dark. We can look at our pictures this time with my new flashlight." They could probably get away with turning on the bedroom light tonight, too, but it would be more fun this way.

She wiggled around, finding a comfortable position. "Carlie, you have to promise you're never going to leave again."

"Of course I'll leave," Carlie answered confidently. "We'll both go off to college, get our own jobs and get married. We can't live together forever, you know."

"Well . . . we'll live nearby, though, and our kids will play together, and our husbands will be best friends. We won't ever move away from each other like Mom and Aunt Janey did."

"No, we'll stay close together," Carlie said. "Maybe I'll marry Jesse. And you'll marry that boy you met, David Henley. We'll teach our kids to play games in the dark."

"Oh, Carlie," Sarah said, feeling excited now. "I can see exactly how it will be." She didn't bother to fold her paper this time—this time, she would need the whole page. "Let's draw the houses where we're going to live someday."

"Okay," Carlie agreed. "Mine's going to have ten rooms."

This wasn't a true game, Sarah thought, because the light from the vent illuminated her paper enough tonight to draw the lines. But that was okay. She wanted this drawing to be done right, with all the lines connecting the way they were supposed to. In the center of the paper, she began by drawing the curve of one of the moons of Jupiter.

Then she drew two space helmets, hers and David's. In the background she placed several domed huts where she and Carlie lived with their families, far away from Earth and Sherman Street. Maybe Kim and Steve Arnold lived there, too. Then she drew a spaceship so they could visit other celestial places. Maybe they would visit Dad and their mother for Christmases and birthdays.

In each dome, Sarah drew two bathtubs and winding stairs going up to the second floor. She drew smiley-faced kids in the bathtubs, kids leaning out the windows and coming out the front doors.

"Okay, let's trade," Sarah said after drawing carefully for a long while. She reached across the space for Carlie's picture and turned on her flashlight dog. Her sister looked grown up tonight, but not quite grown up enough to leave home. That was good.

Sarah pointed the light beam at the paper. Carlie had drawn two houses side by side. Outside each stood a man, a woman and one child. The two women stood close to each other in the middle. They were holding hands.

"Are they us?" Sarah asked.

Carlie nodded. "As soon as the kids go to bed, Jesse and David are going to putter around in one of the garages, and you and I are going to watch television and eat popcorn."

"Popcorn," Sarah said. "A huge bowl, with butter. We'll eat popcorn and drink Cokes and talk until midnight."

Sarah leaned back against the chimney, feeling the warmth of the bricks through her pillow. The food would be from real cupboards, and they'd sit on a soft white couch with lots of pastel pillows. On the walls would be framed photographs of her and Carlie, David and Jesse and all their children.

She stared into the semi-darkness toward the little window at the stairwell. The pictures in her head were more clear now than any she had ever drawn.